Through A Mirror, Darkly

Mary Catelli

Published by Wizard's Wood Press, 2017.

THROUGH A MIRROR, DARKLY

First edition. June 20, 2017.

Copyright © 2017 Mary Catelli.

ISBN: 978-1942564577

Written by Mary Catelli.

Part I

All powers could fly, of course, but not all the same way.

Helen flew like a soaring gull, her arms spread to either side as she crossed the glittering waves, the shoreline barely in sight. Some powers had glamor, danger, and drawing attention the way honey drew flies—and other headaches.

Others—

The sand below subtly shifted ashore and under the waves, and she eased its path this way and that, increasing the width of the beach. Shoals of fish and flocks of birds, dune grass and wild rose, wind-twisted pines farther inland, breezes, the ebbing tide, and ocean currents—all teased at the edge of her awareness, but she kept her attention on the sand. Painstaking, extensive, and far easier than telling the mayor and everyone else who needed to hear that sand and sea shifted, endlessly, and could not be kept in stasis forever, or even for long, so that *they* had no need to change.

Overhead, a thin little cloud blunted the sun's brilliance.

Her phone rang.

With a sigh, she darted ashore. Too much risk of dropping it in the salt water—and besides, she needed to put on more sunscreen. She scowled and closed her eyes to concentrate. No storms raged along shore, and she charged heavily for rescues as the only way to gain some peace.

What could have blown up that couldn't be handled more mundanely than calling her in?

She dropped to the hard sand below the high tide mark and checked the caller.

The Citadel. A cold sliver touched her. Unlikely to be a rescue then. She thumbed the visual. Captain Gale looked anxious—though he brightened at the sight of her.

"Sanddollar—did you hear already? Since you're in your powersuit?"

Her heart sank, but Helen said, sharply, "To keep people from calling the police about a new power—obviously criminal since unknown." Really, he knew as well as any power why they wore suits whenever flying. You couldn't register without one. Just because she did not fight crime. . .

His face turned sternly grave. "How negligent. You should have been the first to be told: Phoebus escaped."

It struck like a blow, as if sunshine had vanished, or birds had ceased to sing. Some powers had nemeses whose plots they had foiled, or who had suffered some injury at their hands. Her? An arrogant blowhard who thought attacking someone who did not train for crime fighting and was vulnerable to his powers best showed off his greatness.

Feeling chilled, she said, "I'll head home at once."

"The Citadel—"

"Is no stronger or more secure than the Cabot house," she snapped. "Daedulus himself said so. *And* it's quicker. I ought to go now and not hang about waiting for Phoebus to attack." Her thumb moved over the off button.

"He still has his stifling collar on," said Captain Gale. "But you know how long that lasts."

Helen nodded.

The shore's quiet almost returned as she put away her phone. The drum of the waves, like the smell of the sea, was too omnipresent to intrude, but her heart hammered. Home, home, she wanted her home, not only for the safety, but to hide away in her nest.

A bird trilled among the brush on the sand dunes. She drew a deep breath and closed her eyes to concentrate. The mist rose slowly from the ocean, but it swathed her.

Not too much, she had to fly quickly, and this unnatural a mist could not be easily raised—and would shout that she was in it. But enough to hide her position and diffuse his attacks.

As soon as the air gleamed swan-white about her, she set off again. At least she did not have far to go, or keep a large area surrounded by the mist to mask her path. She crossed over a pine-laden hill, and a car squatted on the road. A camera swept toward her. She sent mist to engulf him and darted to the left. The route would be longer, but would take her over the marsh, harder to traverse. Her mouth set. Most powers moved into locations like the Citadel, not only for protection from villains, but from weirdoes.

As well, it was best not to give Phoebus too many clues about where she was, she told herself virtuously.

The mist thinned, over the marsh, and something about the landscape ahead of her made her blink. She pulled up in flight and blinked again and again, but she could not put her finger on it. Her gaze went over the scene, back and forth, and after a minute, it dawned on her that the landscape had shifted across an invisible line. And on the other side, everything—the sand dunes, the grasses, the pines, even the sky—all looked subtly darker as well. Not as if a cloud had passed over them, or so little as a haze, because those would have diffused the light. The sunlight had not changed in quality, only lessened. It looked like—

A mirror's reflection.

As soon as she realized that, she saw that every dune, every tree, every blade of grass and hot pink rose had its twin parallel to it. The only thing that was not reflected was herself.

She breathed in and out and still felt light-headed. Something had to affect the light to make it look so faintly dimmer—but this was beyond Phoebus's powers. And he could hardly have bargained with someone while in jail, or out—who else had powers enough to do something like this?

The chess masters, said her thoughts, instantly.

She winced.

All other powers were more or less equal in ability, though arguments could be held. There were no such arguments about the chess masters, who played games with reality itself, and all the people caught in it.

She gulped, closed her eyes, and reminded herself. They would never bargain with Phoebus, or do something for his sake, any more than they would for any other power, hero or villain. They acted as they wished, and they might have done this for their own whim. Again.

The wind pulled at her hair. She should go home and call the Citadel. Whatever little they could do to mitigate the chess masters' deeds was better than nothing.

But the more she had to tell them, the better.

Slowly, she flew to the dividing line, slowing as she approached. It mirrored down to the grains of sand. A wind blew past her. All the grass behind her bent toward the reflection edge, and on the other side, all the grass bent away. Sands cascaded next to her—and on the other side, they cascaded the other way. Sands on this side reached the line and flowed over, without colliding with some wall, or vanishing into nothingness.

She closed her eyes to concentrate. She felt the sand and waves and plants and breeze just as she could on this side.

She drew her breath in and out. It might prove dangerous; she should not linger even without Phoebus threatening, and she certainly should not go in, all the more since no one else knew. But a piece of driftwood, perhaps. . . .

A gull screamed and glided across the line, no more concerned than passing into the shadow of a cloud. Helen bit her lip. It arched its flight back to the other side. And, she noted, it had not been reflected as it flew into sight.

She stepped forward. Walking into the mirrored side produced not even the faintest of sensations.

Which was knowledge enough. She stepped back and took to the air, for swiftness. The line led on and on, and while she never had to cross it on her path, she never flew far from it. She might not even be needed to call it in. Someone had to notice all these reduplicated roses and pines.

Then her house hove into view, and so did its reflection. She swallowed. Sand and grass were one thing, but a house was another. And *her* house, at that.

The reflection, like her own, was long and low, with the faint darker coloring in its beige walls and brown roof being the only sign of difference. She swallowed. Her home.

After a minute, cautiously, she probed the air and sand about it—and started. The air was the same, but the sand held defense stronger than anything she would ever have thought of using. Or else the house had some unfathomable reason for a lot of machinery in the earth about it.

For a moment Helen thought of feeling them out—she could not sense them directly, but with the sand engulfing them, she could work them out negatively—but rejected the notion. She had to go inside.

There, she reached for the phone. Her heart started to hammer harder in her chest. It would be a trick and a half to convince them they needed to prioritize this with Phoebus on the loose, especially when she did not know that it was the chess masters.

She looked out the window at the other house. Her mouth twisted. She knew. She would tell them she would have to investigate on her own if they did not come.

For now, she would remain squarely in her own home. And maybe not even look out the windows after she left one open.

***

Through the open window, he arrived as swiftly as lightning struck. The air sparked when he stopped moving, and Captain Gale, in his suit of electric blue and white, glared at her. She did not get up from her chair.

"If you had only moved to the Citadel when you became a power, we wouldn't have this problem."

"No," said Helen, agreeably. "You'd have a worse one."

He scowled. "They said you babbled about a problem on the phone."

She rolled her eyes. She could hardly move to the Citadel if they couldn't pass on messages better than that.

"Whatever this is, I do not think it's going to improve by being ignored, and no one would have alerted you to *that*."

She pointed out the window. It still took a long minute before his disgruntled expression faded into a flabbergasted blank stare. But the blank stare lasted for a long, long, long time.

"What—the—devil—is—that?"

"Didn't they tell you *anything* I said on the phone? *I—don't—know.* It wasn't there when I left home a few hours ago. Crossing over the line did neither a gull nor me any harm. I didn't feel *anything*. That house has more security than you would believe, all hidden in the sand. And now you know all that I know, none of which will tell you what that is."

Captain Gale managed to turn toward her, however slowly.

"I suspect, of course, the chess masters. But I haven't seen them. I can't tell how large it is, I had to call—and there's a car on the road—"

"That freak who thinks we're Greek gods," said Captain Gale.

For once that was a relief to hear.

"At least it's not the one that thinks we're an alien conspiracy to make the rest of humanity helpless by dependence on us. Moot point, as long as the person didn't cause that." She winced, thinking of another power like the chess masters. "I dodged the camera—that was when I saw—that."

Silence fell. Outside, the breezes bent the grass. After a minute, Captain Gale lifted his phone and began to rap out orders without a glance at her.

Helen drifted over to the window, to watch the scene. Nothing stirred about the other house. Not another Helen, who set security as if she feared an invasion. She shivered, wrapped her arms about herself, and wondered what sort of monsters might dwell on the other side, that might invade.

Or if the other Helen might have given others good reason to invade.

She shivered again. In either case, she herself would have chosen a less—conspicuous hiding place.

She forced her breath out. Captain Gale hung up and, without a glance at her, dialed again. She turned and went for her sunscreen. She would not be staying here long, whether she went in to discover the truth or fled to escape the site. Either way, she would go out into the sun again.

The light in the room shifted, as if windows had been covered, behind her. She turned as Mistress Twilight stepped out of a puff like violet-black shadow. The shadow dissipated behind her, but still she stood like a shadow on the floor, her stygian violet skirts settling about her, a black half mask on her dark face, and her black hair tumbling about her shoulders. Her gaze swept the scene and settled on the window.

She came up beside Helen without looking away. "I *thought* magic would be a problem with the philosophers back."

Phil—Helen's mind went blank for a moment. Then—"You mean the chess masters? You still call them *philosophers*?"

"We're not chess men," said Mistress Twilight, coldly. "Indeed, *they* look more like the pieces. They are not playing chess, therefore, with their—philosophical games."

"They don't look, or act, like lovers of wisdom, either," said Helen.

Captain Gale gave them a bitter glance. "We've got no evidence that it's them. We'll have to keep an eye out for the culprit as well as for Phoebus."

"Who else could do *this*?" said Mistress Twilight.

Helen nodded. "That's like saying there was no evidence that Prankster filled the court house with chartreuse plastic balls. It's like—"

The memory returned like razors—like nightmares—trying to move through the hills when the chess masters had unleashed pure properties at them, so that they were besieged with sensations floating free from any object—of pure bright or bitter or beige or soft or shrill or pungent—and the chess masters had talked of qualia. She had felt like a chess piece in the hand of a player. That had been when she decided against even working with the Citadel. Nevertheless, unpleasant though the thought was—

"Just because they were the first doesn't mean they will be the last," said Captain Gale, flatly. "New powers arise every month if not every week."

"And this new power not only matches their powers—the first time any power has—but just happens to love acting like a philosopher?"

Captain Gale's mouth twitched. "What, you think this shows a great love of wisdom?" Quickly, he walked to the window. "We need to know how large this is. Sanddollar has not seen any edge but this line."

Mistress Twilight raised an eyebrow.

"It exists at least a mile that way." Helen pointed seaward. "I only noticed it coming ashore. I don't know far out to sea it was. Do you see anything about it except that it's magic?"

Mistress Twilight's eyes half closed. After a fearfully silent minute, she shook her head. "Does it go up to the sky, at that? Its height is at least as important as its breadth," she said, opening her eyes.

"First things first," said Captain Gale. Then a sparking trail lead out the door. Except for the faint tracks on the sand, he left no sign, and as soon as he flashed off like lightning, there were not even more tracks.

"Though," murmured Mistress Twilight, "we would hear about satellites if it went too high. Eventually."

The wind slid over the sand, which tumbled, half way between a hiss and a murmur, and obliterated the tracks. For a moment, Helen felt the air and wind, but Captain Gale moved more quickly than was profitable to track—and Mistress Twilight looked intently at her.

"You went through it? To over there?"

"Hopped over and back, nothing more. The birds did more, without even noticing."

After a reflective moment, Mistress Twilight said, "You might check the fish."

"With Phoebus about?" said Helen. "It doesn't seem like his handiwork, but he'd use it—if, indeed, he doesn't try to claim credit for it. And it would be a bit tricky at this distance. I don't want to focus on something like that."

Mistress Twilight raised an eyebrow.

"More support might make it practical." Helen pondered how much force they *could* deploy. Not to mention that they had yet to decide its priority. Living outside the Citadel had that much disadvantage.

Captain Gale darted back within, shedding silvery whiteness. "Miles of it," he said, shortly. "Not into the mountains, barely into the foothills, but still—"

Helen nodded. Still miles.

"Not far out to sea, either. I went around it." He shook his head. "It doesn't have an other side. Not so much as a bit of dark haze. You can just walk through it, and end up looking back at the line and the reflection. And you have to go around to get to the other side."

Helen let her breath out.

"At least it doesn't go too high. Higher than Citadel itself—"

The highest building in the town, Helen noted.

"—and high enough you could have a storm inside, but not much higher, and over it you see land that was there before."

"Never heard of anything like that before," said Mistress Twilight.

"The chess masters have done odder things," said Helen. "The qualia were one."

"And the extension," said Mistress Twilight dryly.

Helen winced. She had not been in the thick of that. Still, the world of raw, exposed extension and charge—she wondered if they had ever figured out *how* the chess masters had managed to inflict such being, unmediated by the senses, on them. Or perhaps just altered all their senses to perceive nothing else.

She plugged on. "But whether this is better or worse entirely depends on what lies inside this—dimension."

"Pocket universe," said Mistress Twilight.

"It—this line—could look as small over there and yet lead to a *full* universe." Then her gaze went over to the other house, and she flinched. She didn't want to know what a full universe would be.

Captain Gale snorted. "If we knew of any other universes, perhaps we could guess. But what you said of that house does not inspire optimism." He shrugged. "We can hope. Perhaps a pirate power or the like bombarded you, and you fled to the Citadel."

And wouldn't you like that, even in another world, thought Helen.

A voice boomed from the dunes. "Hello the house!"

Helen reached for the door leading to the porch.

Lucky Jake, chunky, sloppy in his loose and colorful clothes, with his nut brown hair in havoc from the wind, tromped over the sand. She wondered why he hadn't flown in. Yes, his flight was an inelegant and unsteady thing, but he lurched to and fro as the sand shifted under his feet.

"What's the wonder?" he said jovially.

She pointed. It knocked the grin from his face. Captain Gale ordered him up to the porch and briefed him.

"No one's gone through?" Lucky Jake said, wondering.

"I have," said Helen. "Saw a gull go through, stepped through myself, came back, am fine." She glanced over at her reflected home. "Wasn't right here, though."

Lucky Jake chortled. "Of the three of you—it's *Sanddollar* who's bold enough to try? The one who never fights unless she's back into a corner—and knows more ways out of more corners than she does ways to fight?" He drew himself up to his full height, barely overtopping Mistress Twilight. "Prudent of you. Someone invulnerable is the best scout."

"You sure you don't want to send in the butterflies first?" said Helen dryly.

For someone who bragged of the random grab-bag of powers he had—who claimed not to have been *given* them like all the rest, but to have won them gambling with gods—Lucky Jake blushed easily. Butterfly control being as embarrassing as a clumsy flight, apparently.

After a moment, he said, "I can see what they can see, and no more. What we need is to *fathom* it, and to do things that will tell us more. A butterfly can only see the obvious."

"I see," said Helen gravely.

"It's obvious," said Mistress Twilight, and Helen glanced at her little half smile, and back.

"And I think," said Helen, "that you would be best for it. Since we do not know the danger. I think that house has more defenses than mine—a lot more—but they're not seashore, I can not feel more than their outlines." And hoped he would manage to see more than the obvious.

"Time's a-wasting." Lucky Jake strode back down the steps. The wind tugged his hair and bent the grass so low that it turned silvery, and over the line. Sand hissed over the dunes. Lucky Jake strode on, oblivious to all else, and into the dunes. He plugged on and on, showing no more difficulty than anyone might on the tricky footing.

Helen tensed. Lucky Jake's footsteps vanished into the sand. Any waiting traps could easily be well hidden long before their sandy burial disabled them.

Captain Gale and Mistress Twilight watched with visible calm. Her gaze flickered back to Lucky Jake and beyond. Something metallic and glassy moved in the house's windows.

The explosion startled her, and she leapt through the air. Lucky Jake tumbled through the air, so she reached him in moments, and his face was resigned. Colliding with her, and her bearing him out to the shore, left him sputtering in indignation. He wrenched himself free and bobbed, midair.

"I was safe—I'm immune—"

"To that," spat Helen. "But you were spotted. Something was in the windows. The heavy guns could come into play, and none of us are that immune."

"*You*'re positively fragile," grumbled Lucky Jake.

Mistress Twilight blossomed in midair, like a midnight blue flower. Captain Gale flitted up.

"Wise of you, Sanddollar," he said. "Drawing off the fire this way. No telling what it would do on our side." He shook his head. "I do not like the look of those guns, at all. She expected heavy hitters—"

"You don't know it's a she," said Mistress Twilight. "Just because the house is in the same place doesn't mean it's the same owner."

"It is," murmured Helen, "definitely not the same owner. I can't imagine any court giving me title to it because it's a reflection of mine. Whether it's a like owner—" She spread her hands. "Not very."

"You're private enough," said Mistress Twilight. Helen glared at her.

Captain Gale's mouth twisted. The seabreeze tugged his hair. "We need guards—patrols—things going either way could be trouble, and only powers have any hope of containing it."

"Maybe, maybe not," said Helen. "Too much to learn before we could say that." He eyed her. "Mistress Twilight shouldn't play the messenger. Odds are that magic's involved, and she would be the most likely to recognize it."

Captain Gale lifted his eyebrows. "Take care. Finding things out is no good if you do not get word back."

A moment later, and he was gone.

Mistress Twilight grumbled, "I should check my books."

"If you know enough to recognize this if you find it in a book, I can think of nothing better for you to do," said Helen. "I feel like I'm trying to identify a fish from a single scale."

"It's stygian, and a mirror reflection—that's something." Though her voice was more thoughtful than argumentative.

"Overcast or something," said Lucky Jake, peering upward.

"The light's not just less when it's overcast," said Helen. "It's different. Spread out more. Diffuse. Here it's all from the sun, and you can see it, there's just—less of it."

"Like a reflection," said Mistress Twilight. "In a lake."

"Or—a mirror," said Helen, half lost in thought.

"We should go in," said Mistress Twilight, with abrupt briskness. "We don't know if this is like Wonderland—a lot stranger once you're out of sight of the mirror. They may not have powers, or they may not be able to fly." She lowered herself to the ground.

"Or," said Lucky Jake grimly, "they may recruit them all to work for the government, so we're all breaking the law just by being here."

"Or they are the government," said Helen, the wind whipping about her as she descended, "and we will instantly be inducted into the highest levels of power at once. Let me see something before we find out."

She stood her hands on her hips for a minute. The birds had shifted, the house had changed—she glanced back at where they had come from, where the dunes could be made out.

Her hand went up, and she started to shift the nearest dune, back and farther back.

"What are you doing?" said Lucky Jake.

"Seeing how the reflection works," she said.

The dune merged with the next, first like a dromedary, then, as she pushed on, into one enormous mound. It would not last long like that, even in these breezes, but it would shift how the dunes formed.

"That will test it. I'll be able to see compare the dunes shift here and there. The first of many before I can even consider how to keep things—harmonious about here, between man and nature." Her mouth twisted. "I dare say the chess masters would approve of my testing. Even with a less—fascinating world than when they unleashed those loose properties on us—or were they *qualia*?" She paused. She had heard several explanations, at the time, of how qualia were a person's actual experiences, as of a color; all of which had seemed very abstract. "Did anyone figure that out?"

"Qualia or properties," said Mistress Twilight, severely, her black cloud billowing up about her, "they didn't *shoot* us. The chess masters have never yet been responsible for something lethal. Just things like hippopotamuses appearing out of nowhere."

"They've never been responsible for something lethal *yet*," said Lucky Jake. "But they put us to sleep for a month and gave us dreams we couldn't tell from reality. They just don't care."

He looked at Helen as if to appeal to her. "The world of paper. That was one fun one—you were lucky to miss it, Sanddollar."

"That time," said Helen. "Who knows? They might try the experiment again."

"They've never done that before," said Mistress Twilight.

"Exactly," said Lucky Jake.

Helen let out her breath. The chess masters. The philosophers. The pains in the neck. *She* was stronger than either Lucky Jake or Mistress Twilight, *here*—because as her powers were regional, and she would be far weaker away—a genius loci, they called her. She rubbed the back of her neck. All other powers had about the same level of strength. The chess masters, and the chess masters alone, had powers beyond the range of anyone else. Wherever they went, and whatever they did, they could ignore or strike down leagues of powers. She was beginning to marvel that the Citadel had ever helped against them.

As for ordinary citizens, it was unthinkable.

"I could be dreaming this," said Helen.

Lucky Jake snorted.

"Or you could be, and my dream self said that—you could be the Red King at that—"

Noises broke into her thoughts. Noises like a power battle, flying over the dunes. They would not hear it yet—she stilled the breezes. Over the lap of the waves, the sound made Lucky Jake and Mistress Twilight turn, and Helen swallow. That was a power battle indeed.

"Remember," said Mistress Twilight, as soft as a falling feather, "that we don't know who anyone is, here, and who is innocent, and who is guilty."

"It's coming this way," said Helen. "We can wait and see, without drawing attention by our own flight."

Lucky Jake harumphed and folded his arms, but did not stir.

At least until Butterfly burst over the dunes—lambent in pink, scarlet, and orange, her wings beating the air, her antennae alert on her bald head. Helen jerked to attention, ready to leap, before she remembered. We don't know, she thought, and then, revolted, but it's *Butterfly*, and only the knowledge that the dunes held no children kept her still.

A sideways glance showed her the other two's frozen stances, fighting against motion.

A furred streak leapt upward, entangling Butterfly and brought her face down onto the sand. Wolf, panting hard, pinned her there. His fangs and claws flashed palely in his dark fur. Something feral in his face gave Helen pause. That face would inspire no one to call him the patriarch of the forest.

Laughter followed, low, arrogant—the sort of laughter that—that some adolescent striving to be a big bad villain would long for. She could not imagine who would laugh with such malice. It crawled over her skin like sandpaper.

"Ah, Butterfly, Butterfly." Cherubim flew up. Helen blinked. But Cherubim it was, flaming sword in hand, six vast wings as multi-colored as an opal flapping at the breeze as he lazily flew up. He all but purred at her. "Did you really think it would do any good, this distraction?"

Helen glanced sideways. Even in her gloom, Mistress Twilight looked pale with shock—as Cherubim did not. Lucky Jake gawked. Heaven help us, Helen thought.

"They're already rounding up the children." Wolf smiled, baring all his fangs. "This time, you will not shelter them."

Some things were clear in themselves, if perplexing in content. Helen shot up into the air, surveying the dunes, and seeing no allies of theirs. She swept down again. Her hands rose, and she blasted up sand from the dunes, to strike both of Wolf and Cherubim in the chest, and drive them back.

Lucky Jake whooped behind her and bounded to the attack. Mistress Twilight—but she kept up a sandy barrage and could not look, could not see more than that Mistress Twilight moved. Screaming abuse, Cherubim hurled himself at her, and she sent wind whirling and him tumbling through the air. Not that she could easily guess what a spell did, not like Lucky Jake's pummeling of Wolf. She had to trust Mistress Twilight to do something useful.

Cherubim wiped sand from his face, glanced to one side. Despite herself, Helen glanced over. Butterfly had vanished.

"She's broke for it!" bellowed Cherubim.

Wolf, with a great surge, broke free and bounded off, snarling every inch of the way.

Helen hesitated. They still knew nothing more than the malice of those two. Lucky Jake must have thought the same, standing and watching their escape.

Gloom blossomed like a rose, and Mistress Twilight reappeared. After a silent moment, Butterfly emerged in pink and ruby to stare. Particularly, Helen noted, at her. She thought. The woman's gaze jerked about a lot, like—her mouth twisted—a butterfly's loopy path, but less happily.

"No matter," she said, her voice soft and ragged, "no matter how mad the world is—has become—this I do not believe."

"Where are the children?" said Helen, fighting down a sudden nausea and trembling. That fight, on top of this—she had heard of Butterfly's crimes—but Lucky Jake and Mistress Twilight might have been among those who found the bodies. Perhaps Cherubim—this Cherubim—had lied. Honest as the day was long, was Cherubim, but he would not laugh like that.

And she could not prejudge, not in this, not after what Wolf said, and how Cherubim had acted—

Butterfly raised her head proudly. "As if I would tell you!"

Helen's voice grew dry. "Has anyone made you a better offer, to protect them?"

Butterfly opened her mouth and shut it again.

"You seemed rather desperate there. You might have to take desperate risks of a different stripe to help them."

Butterfly closed her eyes, and despair washed across her features. But what she said was, "Follow me."

***

She had to go ahead of the three of them, at that, to lure them out of their hiding place. They could see a bobbing bit of pink and scarlet, now and again, but the low, wind-twisted pines often hid her, and Helen could only uneasily think they were losing their best clue to this world.

"If she comes out blood-splattered," grumbled Lucky Jake, lingering in her side vision, "don't say I didn't warn you."

"You didn't warn us," said Helen without a glance aside. "Warnings have to be delivered in advance far enough that we can act upon them. *You* are just making a dismal prediction."

Lucky Jake grumbled but did not argue.

Then the colorful patch flew toward, and seven people followed, five children and two women—all pasty pale, grimy, glancing about constantly, and dressed in clothes faded, ragged, and never having been too pricey at their best. The children scurried close to the women. One child saw Helen, squeaked, and hid behind one woman, and all the rest stopped, their eyes large, as if only fear of flight kept them from running away.

"Is that all of them?" said Helen, mildly.

"And," said one woman, "I thought things had gone mad *earlier*."

Butterfly nodded. "But Sanddollar fought on the same team as the other two—something has happened. Something mad."

"They'll be more mad, shortly," said Helen. "If you want them safe as well, you want to move quickly." She glanced at Mistress Twilight.

"I don't want to move them through," said Mistress Twilight. "Not here, not when we do not know—" She spread her hands.

"Afoot is quick enough, it isn't far." Helen winced. Into her home. There was not another defensible structure for far too far. Evacuate later, when they had more support—"I can take one of the kids."

"And I," said Lucky Jake, "can take three."

***

With one child perched on his shoulders and one tucked under either arm, Lucky Jake swung along the sand with insolent ease.

The little girl riding piggyback on her was quiet and still, but Helen was wondering if she were quite up to it. (And after Lucky Jake had taken the bigger children!) She looked about.

"There it is." Her house looked both a better refuge than ever before, and farther away, as if transported to the moon. It was perhaps the nearer one that did it. "We'll still have to go around—"

Someone flew over the ocean toward them. Helen pulled back among the dunes. Mistress Twilight's gloom seeped about them. The flyer paused in midair, despite her arms outstretched like a gull's, and glared down

A pale-haired woman wearing a costume of sea-blue—with a golden sanddollar just visible at this distance. Helen's breath hissed out, and Lucky Jake whispered, "Sanddollar, that's you!"

"Keep on moving," she said, and hoped her voice did not shake. No time to think—she could only hope that Mistress Twilight could use this knowledge. "We'll have to keep an eye on her."

One woman stepped up silently and took the girl from her back. "You'll need to be free if you fight."

"Best if we don't," said Helen. Mist puffed up, whiter than a swan's wing, about them; she had a moment's glance at Butterfly's face, and that of the women, and no time to wonder at their bafflement. "Onward. Quickly." Despite the loose sand, but they had no choice. "She could put down the mists again, no doubt."

As if she had reminded her, the breezes rose, as unnaturally as the mist, as they plugged onward—for a time. Then the breezes were still again, and when they burst from the mist on her doorstep, she could see no sign of the other Sanddollar.

She swept them all onto the porch, behind its screens, and its more subtle defenses. Pulling the door shut, she realized how they all stared.

"You. You of all people," said Butterfly, slowly and wonderingly. "Not only having allies but avoiding a fight."

"Stay here," she said crisply. "We are going to get even more allies because I do not think that even I will be able to prevent all fights." She hurried past to check the security systems. Designed against trespassers mostly—she had no doubts that they did nothing against the chess masters—but it would help against anything past the line. Like that Sanddollar.

She shuddered. They would have to ask them what they meant by their surprise, but that Sanddollar gave her a few hints.

Mistress Twilight was on the phone when she returned. Lucky Jake sat on a couch, eyeing the little crowd that clumped in the corner. Even Butterfly seemed as quiet and cowed as the women and children. Helen supposed that she might have difficulty controlling four adults and five children at once, whatever pheromones she used.

None of them looked outside.

Mistress Twilight hung up, and her voice was crisp. "They've already got the patrols up. They'll send more here to protect against *her*." Her thumb jabbed out to point at the reflected house. Helen hoped that her reclusive style—after that surprise at her having allies—meant she aimed more for defense than offense.

"I warned them to be particularly wary of people who looked familiar. Captain Gale warned me to keep you here—Phoebus is still about, and they have reports his collar is off."

"Hope so," said one boy, so softly that Helen thought she could pretend not to hear it.

"Well," she said, "if I can't go out, I'd best see what I could do in." Groceries, she thought. Mistress Twilight could do a grocery run if it came to that, though; they would not suffer passing through the gloom.

She turned to face her guests. One girl hid behind her mother.

"You said that everything went mad. When was this?"

"Morning," said the smallest child.

"Sun was all up," said the second smallest. "We were down by the beach. We were playing. . . ." Then he sat with a bump and started to wail in the middle of the floor.

Butterfly surged forward to take up him up and pat his back. "It was nine. I was in town, the church bells rang—four times—cut off halfway." She frowned. Her voice slowed, as if the words were reluctant to come. "I can only suppose the bellringer was murdered. So—so many murders."

"So much blood," said one woman.

Pale faces all about nodded.

"So many murderers," said the other woman. "They all hated each other, but the world went mad. . . ." She shuddered. "Arson, destruction, and more murder. The world went mad."

Maybe it had, thought Helen, looking from one face to the next. Maybe not. "We think that the chess masters—"

Butterfly's bitter laughter broke in. "Tried again? I have to give them credit for trying, so humanely, but they've never persuaded anyone to the straight and narrow yet—" Her eyes narrowed. "Up to now," she said, more sedately. "What in blue blazes happened to the notorious Sanddollar? Out to foment conflict wherever she could?"

Sanddollar's mouth worked.

"Between man and nature, specially," said the tallest child, solemnly. "Because it preserved only the fit."

"But if they unleashed *you* in their moral efforts," said Butterfly, "what was *she*?" Words seemed to fail her.

Words did not come to Helen in the first place, until finally, noting there were larger, and more rapid, threats to harmony than erosion, she managed to say, "I think I need to call the conservancy. Let them know I won't be refurbishing sandbanks any time soon."

***

Helen checked the security again, and when she came out, drew away Lucky Jake and Mistress Twilight, out to the dunes—explaining, out of earshot, that she wanted to see what they would do if they thought they were unobserved.

Then she drew a deep breath. "I don't think they *existed* before nine am."

The breeze blew over the dunes, making the grass bow down.

When neither Lucky Jake nor Mistress Twilight contradicted her, she plowed on. "It's like a world where everything's the opposite of us. But once it exists, it could *act* the opposite. And since we don't go around butchering each other on the streets—" She spread her hands.

Lucky Jake snorted. "And what is your opposite doing now?"

Silence lasted. Helen looked at the house, nervously. Whatever her opposite had—and out of sight, she had more defense—she knew her own. "I have alarms that would alert me if—she—moved."

"Is she trying to do anything with powers?" said Mistress Twilight.

Helen drew a deep breath and closed her eyes.

"We need to know—" began Lucky Jake.

"Good thing you have me," said Helen. "Though it's going to take me a minute, and the two of you have to be quiet."

She reached out through sun-warmed air and deep sandy depths, and rose roots holding on the earth and lifting up flowers for bees, and the rhythmic lap of the sea waves as the tide turned.

The shift was so deep that she would not have felt it without taking in the entire view, but deep in the sands, a force gathered for attack, and overhead, clouds and winds alike stirred with discord.

"Such discord," she whispered. Then she opened her eyes.

"Inside," she said. "Get the refugees into the basement. Call HQ and tell them we're facing an attack by—" Both Mistress Twilight and Lucky Jake looked at her with flat expression. "—by, well, me. Call the Weatherman and tell him that she's doing a storm."

"He won't like that," said Lucky Jake.

He wouldn't. For a man who began as a villain threatening storm and flood, he had remarkably little tolerance for other weather malefactors—or just weather modifiers. But she had survived his rage before.

"The sooner we contain it the better, then." She started toward the house herself, lurching over the uneven footing when the sand slipped, barely evading the roses and their thorns, but she could not lose her awareness as she tried to plot her counterattack. Reversing, she might manage but—her tongue touched her lips—this other Sanddollar would likely match her in strength. Wiser to divert it and husband her strength.

Only—to divert it required mastering its path and working out where it could be diverted. Which would give *her* plenty of time to gather force.

Gregor, she thought as she walked up the steps. She needed Gregor's help. Better to divert her attack than to face off with someone *exactly* as powerful as she was.

Or rather, Geometry. In the field, she should call him by his code name.

Captain Gale would no doubt insist on evacuating the women and children. Her mouth twisted. Wise of him. Then they would be his problem.

Wind ruffled the grass. It felt colder than the sun should have allowed.

The Weatherman had, perhaps, unremarkably little tolerance for weather malefactors, she thought.

***

Geometry's gaze looked unfocused, as it so often did, and the air about him seemed to hold a miasma of sharp angles and smooth arcs. The breeze, coming over the dunes, tugged at his hair oddly, passing through that geometric cloud at odd angles. Even knowing they were illusions of the purest kind, Helen held her breath. If Geometry needed her help, he'd ask for it. The only thing she might be able to do was point out the powers—gathering, building in the earth and air and sea even as he worked—to direct him. It wasn't as if their powers were miscible. Pure geometry shifting in space. Only when he had thus set the paths could she use them to move things.

About the house, far off, other powers flew, surveying—avoiding the other Sanddollar's lands as if they were poisoned.

Captain Gale darted through the grass, spraying sand, and came up beside her. Lucky Jake and Mistress Twilight came down from the porch. Helen inched backwards, hoping to give Geometry more room.

His gaze still intent on Geometry, Captain Gale said, his voice low, "It's not that large. As deep as it is wide, and it only goes out a bit to sea, and up to the mountains."

"And then it ends?" said Helen. She tried, for a moment, to envision it.

"Well—then it blurs into black mists, with nothing moving. Bitterly cold."

Lucky Jake lifted his eyebrows. "Monsters coming out?"

"None that I saw," said Captain Gale, soberly. Wind ruffled his hair.

"Then it's time for a rescue," said Helen. "If only we had known sooner, we could have acted sooner. There must be more innocents than those who escaped."

"There must have been," said Mistress Twilight, soberly. She glanced at the cellar. "When it was created."

"Some might have hidden. Or those trying to kill them were killed themselves. Or someone tried to enslave them instead. At least we have limits to who faces us." An equality of power did not always mean an equal fight, and she started to reel off the escapes. "No Weatherman, or Daystar, or Arete, or Errata, or Thunderbird—"

"She's moving!" called Geometry, and all of them turned, questions of rescue shoved aside. Helen's heart pattered the faster as she reached out to test the other Sanddollar's plan. That came before all rescues; if they could not retreat, they could not rescue.

The air felt electric and ready to strike. Helen hesitated. She had never felt such force except in a natural storm. Certainly she could not rouse such a storm, let alone that swiftly.

Delicately, she probed at the air, shifting this breeze and that one, brushing on electric current and diverting them. They flew easily down arced paths through the air.

The wind boomed, and the air shook, resolving into harsh laughter. And then speech.

"That is what you pit against me? A weak and pitiful resistance?"

Helen looked up. Herself, framed in lightning, floating on the air, her face contorted with fury and her hair flying so wildly in the choppy wind that it looked like writhing snakes, looked back. The sanddollar on her sea blue shirt was plain enough—Helen could not see whether it was darker than her own in this lighting—and the power about them built, in air and sand.

"A pathetic, shadowy non-entity!"

Helen grabbed Geometry's arm. "Shoot things right and left," she said, urgently. "I'll direct them to move."

Geometry lifted an eyebrow, but Helen could only hope he listened. Softly she urged the sands and air and lightning to motion.

"You fool—I judged you rightly! You are weak! You prattle of harmony when strength comes from conflict!" She laughed harshly. "You *whisper* of harmony—I had to listen on breezes to hear your lies—when I am bold enough to shout the truth!"

Sand flooded toward her with titanic blows. For a paralyzed moment, it stunned her with its violence. Then, frantically, she started to shove, forcing the sand away.

And away. And away. Sand rose in great enormous heaps that she could see only out of the corner of her eyes—she certainly could not turn her head to even look. She ached all over from the effort to push—

Then, abruptly, it stopped. Every muscle in her body ached. She had never even dreamed of moving so much sand, and this reflection of hers had done it so easily.

"So! Weakling! You call for *help!*"

Still aching, Helen glanced about. Past the heaped sand, flights of powers came surging over sand dunes.

The other Sanddollar darted off, faster than Helen could have flown after her.

Numbly, Helen looked at the enormous mounds of sand. It overtopped her house and engulfed all that grown where it landed. She started to shift it back where it came from—and found that she started to tremble.

She drew a deep breath and went to work more slowly. It did not stop the tremble. She would stage no rescue for a time.

Part II

On the screen, Phoebus gleamed more radiantly than ever, his blond hair and glittering costume arranged to reflect the light. Must have practiced, she thought, and felt cold. His face was a rictus of fury.

Captain Gale waved at the image. "And that's why you shouldn't exert yourself. Phoebus is being upstaged. He's not pleased. Any more than he was when you first undid him."

"Again," said Helen. A truck rumbled up toward the house. Helen did not glance out. They shuffled off the women and children—and Butterfly, who seemed as stunned and in need of shelter as the rest. Perhaps more.

"So we need you to stay put. Hard enough to protect you with this happening—"

"Why?" said Mistral, with more surliness even than normal. She slumped in a living room chair. "If Sanddollar had let us *train* her, she'd fight off Phoebus and this too. By herself. Like the powerhouse she is."

"She's got her weakness," said Lucky Jake from the kitchen, not looking up from his sandwich. "It all balances out—"

"Oh yes," said Mistral, "she can only fly, she can't work away from the shore—which she never leaves!" She tossed her head, and her shimmering gray hair rose on a breeze that moved nothing else in the room.

"Good thing, that," said Helen acidly. "Who knows how far this thing would have flourished before someone thought to call it in?"

Mistral muttered under her breath. Something about encouraging powers to go off and live by themselves. As if, thought Helen, there was ever a genius loci who did not love his home ground.

Captain Gale shifted his weight. "It's not growing. Shades off into dark mists that don't look pretty but they aren't moving out."

"Or in?" said Helen.

He nodded. "Or in. I have a device for surveying such things. Dr. Mechanism made very sure it could calculate things down to the millimeter."

"No monsters?" said Lucky Jake, grinning, from the kitchen doorway, his hands full of sandwich.

This place, thought Helen, sourly, makes much better home than it does a meeting place for powers. At least she could still retreat to her bedroom for privacy.

"No formless creatures of mists and gloom?" Lucky Jake went on.

"No," said Captain Gale calmly. "Just standard shape mists."

His mouth full of sandwich, Lucky Jake blinked.

"At any rate," said Helen, "we know they are now. That other Sanddollar could do more with such shapes and such mist, perhaps." For a moment, she wondered how much more *she* could do with the mists—but she had no time now. "We need to scout and save what we can. The women and—" She hesitated. "Butterfly reported insanity, chaos, and slaughter—but who knows who escaped alive in the confusion? We'd have to separate fighters in frays before establishing which side we support."

She ran a hand through her hair. "On the bright side, it looks limited. No duplicate Weatherman, or chess masters, or Golden Man."

"What the problem there?" said Mistral. "I'm sure a *reflected* Golden Man would be a model of generosity and indifference to wealth."

"What? He'd force it into our hands?" said Helen.

Lucky Jake snorted and swallowed. "In such excess that we could not fly, no doubt."

Captain Gale said, "We should survey and be sure of whom we face. As soon as we see your refugees off."

***

"We're supposed to believe *that*?" said the driver. He glared at Butterfly, who looked meek and mild and innocent. Helen remembered seeing Butterfly—the other one—in many a pose of virtue, but injured innocence and eternal patience was new.

She swallowed. She hoped nothing untoward would happen on the way—she had just guessed that the effect would mirror her—and what with Butterfly's vicious crimes—

"I ain't got the security to deal with her. Just this morning—you shoulda watched the news!" He waved in irritation toward the other house. "Not even that would drive off what *she* did. They are still trying to find her and this time's kid—"

One child from the mirror side was scowling so hard that she thought he would hit the driver.

"Butterfly," said Helen, sharply, "where were you this morning at nine?"

"Nine?" Butterfly's hand waved. "I did not know at once about the—this—I was underground, in a hideout, there was—" She frowned, looked bewildered.

"Nevermind what there was." Butterfly, thought Helen, had not thought through what the mirror meant for the original, or how people would react to her about children. "Mistress Twilight, take her to town. Have her lead the police to the hideout."

Butterfly looked at her with mild eyes.

"Use your powers if you must, Butterfly," said Helen. "Even on the police. There's a kid's life at stake. Bet you you'll find the other one still there."

Mistress Twilight flinched. The gloom started to arise about her.

Captain Gale shifted. "Give her an id bracelet."

Butterfly looked between them. Mistress Twilight stepped forward and took her wrist.

"You will be glad to have moved as swiftly as you could," said Mistress Twilight. Darkness engulfed them, and they were gone.

That, thought Helen, at least settled the question of getting her away. The women and children gaped, and Helen went to usher them toward the van.

No sooner than it trundled away, sending sand flying, than Captain Gale said, "Patrols are all very well, but you were right, Sanddollar—we need to survey the interior, get a census if we can." He looked at her. "All shoreline, we know that. Would have been best if you had drilled with us, but you are the only one I *know* should go in."

Helen shifted her weight, wondered if Mistral had told the truth about her training, and said, "Send in someone with shadow powers, too."

"Sent in Shade. You know what Shade's like."

Her mouth twisted. Like everyone else, she knew how little she knew about Shade, because Shade liked privacy. More to the point, Shade would go unseen unless needed—and maybe even then.

She felt very alone.

"Did you have any prisoners?" she said.

He frowned but shook his head. "Last ones were a week ago; plenty of time to ship them off to the Super-max."

"Good."

Dryly, he said, "They—their reflections—would be good, you know."

"And prisoners. Of people who would not be good—in general, or to them. I fear for any hero caught in there."

***

In the reflection, the chapel stood where it stood on the other side. Helen flew slowly over the strand and studied it. Mary, Star of the Sea. Except that she was as certain as she had ever been of anything, that the chapel would not be that.

She flew by, not glancing aside, but the corner of her eye picked out a sullen red star, and a death's head. She shuddered. Even turning her face away, she could not help notice the roses growing in the dunes about it. The blooms were not the clear sunrise pink of the other side, but a dark red, almost black, far darker than the reflection itself would explain. The thorns were larger, and sharper, and more plentiful, than on any rose she had ever seen before.

Onward, she told herself. To the city. She picked up speed in her flight.

Buildings started to appear, cottages as they were on the other side. Painted pastel shades, and most bleached an even paler hue, and only darker than the cottages on her side the way the rest of the reflection was. Some had little gardens about them, and she felt a bit uneasy about the flowers, and the garden art.

Then she smelled smoke.

It rose from a ruined cottage, which a blazing fire had reduced little more than one soot-covered wall. Her mouth tightened, and she forced herself to verify that there were no visible bodies.

She flew on. More ruins. The burnt-out ones could be seen the most easily, and left the air always scented with smoke, but others looked as if they had been savaged by construction equipment. Not quite complete-ly—as if boredom had kept the devastation from being thorough. Some, she thought, had been torn apart by high winds.

The bodies were less evident. Sprawled in odd corners, under trees or brushes, inside wreckage. . . . Helen flew a little higher and told herself it was to see farther, to take in more of the scene, rather than to obscure detail.

A few people skulked about. More, indeed, were in fist fights than moving about. Some waved their fists at her, screaming. She shifted the air to carry the sound and learned they were not cursing her for failing them, but demanding that she come down and fight.

She summoned a little mist to obscure her from sight. Her path carried her over the streets where the shops began, where a bank stood. . . .

"Ha! You emboldened yourself!" The voice was clear and ringing, aided by powers to reach here. "There would be hope for you yet, if I weren't going to end it and you!"

Knowing what she would see, dreading it every second, Helen turned toward the bank and the voice. Hanging over the building was the other Sanddollar. She had arrayed herself in black and blood red that did not suit her. And hacked her hair short. With a butcher's knife, apparently, and with her eyes closed, it was so ragged.

And her face was so wild and avid that Helen almost expected to see blood on her teeth as she grinned.

"I will hold no more to those foolish, wan colors but bright and brilliant ones. To strike fear. As I foment the troubles that will make the world stronger!"

Air started to stir, and the breezes strengthened by the moment. The other Sanddollar herself did not move. Just kept her gaze on Helen.

Helen drew a deep breath and roused the fog.

Panic must have helped. Whiteness flooded up, engulfing her and all the city—and neither she nor the the other Sanddollar could detect each other, not being seaside beings. No one could see through this pea soup. A few profane shouts rose as fights became impossible.

Get out, she told herself. The other Sanddollar could find all the flying things that were not seashore beings by the void they left, and her talents were not suited to capture at the best of times. She reached out as far as she could, trying to sense the shore. The buildings and the people would at least appear as voids, and the other Sanddollar would have act through it—

"YOU FOOL!"

The shout resounded painfully through the mists. Helen flinched. Wood moaned about her from the force of the sound wave. She could feel how the other had manipulated the winds to do it, but she had not felt her gather the power. She shifted away as slowly and subtly as she could.

"DO YOU THINK TO STOP ME?"

The wind picked up. Briskly. Helen summoned mist and more mist, but sand stung her, and the wind buffeted her along—not just from the wind shifts that warned her to evade buildings—she had to evade several and told herself that the other could not pick her out, or she would face far more—

She frowned and picked out the other Sanddollar by the way the winds surged about her; the other gaps in the air were buffeted as she was. For a moment, she appraised the winds, then, grabbing and twisting them, she set a blast of sand toward the other Sanddollar.

She felt the sand hitting, and the winds abruptly subsided. The mists did not thicken much farther. She threw herself north, for the easiest path to pure shoreline, where she could sense all.

Then the winds rose up again, swiftly. A great blast bore her out of the mists.

"Do you think you can hide from me?" bellowed the other Sanddollar.

Helen seized the air. For a moment, she stilled it. Then, her thoughts tumbling over each other, she stirred the air beside her, making it sound as if she were flying to her right. Flying rather swiftly. . . .

A blast of sand shot through where she had put the noise. Helen instantly stilled the air to silence.

"That showed you," said the other Sanddollar, the air redolent with her gloating. "That showed you."

Helen pulled away. She could have realized that something was wrong by the way there was a woman-sized hole where she could not feel the air, but she would not throw away this chance, all the more in that she did not think she could blast back like that.

The winds gusted again, as if the other Sanddollar sought another foe, and she tumbled over the docks, which were not empty.

Captain Gale had warned her. Phoebus had been on the docks at nine.

Gulls screamed, and flotsam and jetsam smelled, heavily, on the air. She did not turn aside. A fair-haired man, his glittery clothes torn and begrimed, skulked in the corners, behind weathered buildings and crates.

He was not fighting, which would be the final clue. Except, she reminded herself, he might fight someone from her side, so that she could not be sure whether he was hero or villain regardless of whom he fought, until one or the other showed true colors.

Best to be wary for both.

Slowly, Helen flew downward, to settle on the dock. As if she approached a frightened kitten—as if there were any chance at all that her appearance would not alarm him.

The softness of her landing did not keep Phoebus from hearing it. He looked over and jumped back. Then he started to edge away.

From the air, she had underestimated how bruised and bloodied he was. He, unlike the one on her side, still had a stifling collar about his throat, so she did not have to fear his powers. He eyed her like a beast in a trap.

For a fleeting moment, she imagined he was Phoebus in truth, already slipped over to this world. She forced her breath out. Phoebus's conceit would not let him slip away, even with the collar, and she doubted he could have gotten it back and gotten this injured since Captain Gale's news.

He was already edging away, and she could not let this little world slaughter all within. And if she took forever, the other Sanddollar would kill them both.

"Stay still," she said, as soothingly as she could. His eyes looked calculating, but he did not move.

Half the superheroes she knew could deal with a collar more easily and more quickly than she could. Captain Gale could short it; Daystar could tear it off; Wolfe could shred it. But—a little water condensed *here*, and *here*, and *there* —her eyes closed as she tried to short it out—salt water would be better perhaps—and then the collar hissed. Phoebus yanked it off. He stood there, staring at it, unspeaking. Helen wondered how to urge him along when he was still in shock.

His voice, when he managed to speak, was hoarse. "Now I know the world has gone mad."

Helen drew her breath in and out. "Since this morning?"

He flinched. Then his gaze went behind her and fixed.

She turned her back on him, only realizing as she did so that she did not think it a risk, and only briefly. Cherubim, Wolfe, and Lucky Jake charged them. From the pure hatred on their faces, the side they came from was clear.

Her hands flew up, summoning a thick mist, to buy them moment, before even she realized how battered and bloodied they were. Easier to fly off, then, she told herself—and quickly—that mist would barely slow Wolfe—

"Look away," said Phoebus.

She obeyed. And still blinked at the flare of swan-white radiance behind them.

"Now—escape!"

They soared over choppy waves and into the head wind. Shouts of fury resounded behind them, and moments later, the sounds of fighting. They had blamed each other. Well, it was safer that way, but she still shivered.

Phoebus frowned and pulled up. A dark haze rose ahead them, and she quickly calculated. Yes, this was where Captain Gale had seen the edge.

They could not count on the fight lasting, or killing all three of them, or Phoebus's light having left them blind and unable to pursue.

"This way." She turned out to sea. There might be ships, there might be powers, but it had to be safer than land.

The other Phoebus flew alongside. "Are the chess masters responsible?"

For a moment, Helen envisioned a mirrored chess master. Then she said, demurely, "We have our suspicions."

He shook his head. "They mean well."

Even with all the perils of this place, she turned to look at him.

He sounded exhausted, but the words just tumbled out of him. "Even with the qualia, and the naked extensions—they speak so eloquently and exhaustively—but sometimes I wish they were less willing to regard themselves as our moral equals and *use* their powers. Maybe—" He shook his head.

There did not seem to be any good answer to that—and flying on would mean leaving. She banked back toward the shore. Phoebus followed wordlessly for long minutes, but as the sand appeared ahead, he said, shortly, "You mined that."

"*She* mined that," said Helen, equally shortly. "I'm not the one you know." So to speak, she thought. She wondered if it could be called knowledge when his memory created with the rest of him. "Let's hide."

A little clothing shop, mostly catering to tourists. The mines could not reach that far. For a moment, she wondered how the other Sanddollar mined the land without leaving traces that would make it not a perfect reflection, but then she snored. Smoothed the sand over, of course. She could have done it herself.

Over sand and dunes and tall grass and flowering roses, she flew, to land on the road. They could walk to the shop. For a moment, she hoped that the store had not had anyone there, or that at least, it had not opened. They might not find bodies. But first—

Phoebus landed behind her. The sea breeze tugged at his hair a minute, and his face bore a solemn expression that she had never seen on the face of her old enemy.

He met her gaze. "Can you deaden the air about us? So we can't be heard?"

Her eyebrows went up—but she supposed they did have the same powers. "Earth, too—enough to talk and nothing more."

He drew a deep breath and studied her.

"And I have," she added dryly. "That's why there is no breeze."

"What's happening? What have they done this time? It's a night-mare!" His hands shifted in midair. "Dozens of burglaries at once—I knew they were all crooks, but they killed each other in the end! And Argent started a slaughter—it's not going to be a town after this—" He drew a deep breath. "And then *you*."

"I'm not the one you knew," she repeated. Or don't know—the one you think you know. "Something—happened."

"What?" He took a step toward her and seized her hand as if afraid she would vanish if he did not.

"I—think—that you—" She licked her lips. "I think that you did not actually exist before this morning. About nine."

He blinked. His grip slackened, fractionally.

"I think that the chess masters used some kind of mirror magic to cre-ate a mirror world, reflecting part of ours—of reality. You were reflected. Created in your entirety." She swallowed. "Including all your memories."

For a moment, he blinked again, as if her words had made no sense at all. Then, slowly, blood drained from his face.

"Argent is a great hero on our side, like Cherubim. Lucky Jake is a great guy, if not so great a hero. So's Wolfe—a bit rough, but friendly. I would never *dream* of mining the shore—and I suspect you can guess what our chess masters are like. Cold. Distant. Silent. Unconcerned. Just the sort of people who would do this."

For a moment, she wondered if they had been reflected as well. But no, the reflections would have acted by now, in the face of this evil; the chess masters had kept themselves without a reflection to help against them.

Phoebus's colorless lips moved. "And I? What sort of man do *I* reflect?"

Helen's mouth opened and shut, and opened again, before she had words. "What is your name?"

He gave her a sharp sideways glance. "Jack Smith."

"Was it always?"

He flushed a little and looked down. "It used to—my parents named me Apollos Aurelius Worthington. Too high-faluting fancy for words."

She took both his hands. It was remarkably easy to think of him as Jack.

"The man you are a reflection of was born Jack Smith and changed it to Apollos Aurelius Worthington. For a name worthy of him."

His eyes closed, screwed shut, and he shook his head.

"We have to get you new clothes."

His eyes popped open, and he looked down at the dirt, blood, and tatters. "It's not—"

"Or you'll be taken for him. He likes that sort of getup." After a moment, she said, softly, "Why do *you* wear something that gaudy?"

His mouth opened, and shut again.

"Well," she said, as briskly as she could (and that was not very, she realized), "better that you reverse his morals than his clothes, however rare it is."

"So that's why I wear this," he murmured, as if he had forgotten she was there. He shook his head. "Yes, I want to change."

"I think that everything that would make it look different did not change So—there's a store here. With clothes."

She pointed. Ahead, the sand dunes turned to something like earth (though she could still feel the sand in it), and pine trees grew thickly, though gnarled by the winds. In the midst of a grove stood a store, with a porch, all built of weather-beaten wood.

He nodded.

They had not crossed much of the distance before she realized she had hoped in vain. Bodies lay strewn over the porch, and one over the threshold. Two rocking chairs lay, broken, and a checkers board had been overturned from the top of a barrel. Black and red pieces sprawled over the porch, down to the earth, and into the puddles of drying blood.

Helen swallowed. The old men had never cared much about winning, on the other side. For the first time, she had come so close, and could, despite the scent of pine needles, smell the corpses. . . .

"The living come first," said Helen, half to herself. Then she straightened and swallowed, hard, again. Jack still looked at the bodies. "And you need to keep from starting a fight yourself. Everyone with powers is needed. Picking clothes unlike you wear now will confuse the issue long enough for us to talk."

Slowly, he nodded. "Inside. Make sure there are no others, still alive."

She bit her lip and looked at the doorway.

Jack pulled open a window and flew inside. She followed, and they swiftly surveyed the place. Few places to hide.

"I'll watch," she said, and snatched a bottle of water from the frig. "Make sure no one sneaks up."

She paused only behind the bushes outside, her stomach heaving up her breakfast, and to wash out her mouth. Moments later, she sat on the roof. Birds cheeped and twittered, invisible in the trees. The sun was radiant, and the only thing that kept the scene before her from beauty was its blandness.

No human figures, which was just as well. Jack—those women and children—how long could any survivors last in this? Good or evil?

"Ready," said Jack, beside her. She turned. Clean of blood, though still bruised. Dressed in pale blue jeans, and a plain white t-shirt. The wind tussled his straw-blond hair, and her mouth went dry.

"Will this do?" he said.

"Yes. No one will have trouble tell you apart. Let's—"

His gaze went past her, and his mouth eased.

She turned. A small, rotund robot, in gaudy colors, hung before them, turning black lenses to focus on them. She took a step back before she remembered that she could not tell the reflection from the original. A shade darker, perhaps, but she could not be sure. Especially with the few times she had seen the robot before.

Jack, at least, was not afraid. Then, perhaps he had not had the time to consider what the origin of the reflection would be like.

The voice was the same—cold, mechanical, enough to convince that the speaker was emotionless. She had seen enough of imp to know the danger of thinking that.

"How can I help you?"

A bark of laughter escaped her. That would be what imp would say, certain that it could help by overturning their lives, introducing uproar and chaos, and their abuse was the most certain sign of its success in liberating them—

"This is no time to be laughing," said the floating robot. "Disorder is everywhere."

She choked down more laughter. Easier than she would have guessed—imp would never have said that.

"That was a test. There is some order to this chaos." She turned to Jack. "I will get some metal paint. You tell it what I told you."

"Paint?" said the robot.

Jack gestured at his clothes. "It's needed to avoid a superfluous fight. You will need a quick paint job, too, mender."

***

Mender, mender, mender. She repeated it to herself as Jack painted, with care. He could only do so much, since they could not endanger mender's functionality with paint in the wrong place; mender might be needed, as much as Jack, as well as any hero who might fight them.

"Jack?" she said. He glanced over. "What did you call yourself here? As a hero?"

"Phoebus," he said, without hesitation.

She nodded, slowly. Gusts of wind buffeted her. "And the other—me is Sanddollar?"

"She sounded like she's going to change that," said Jack, dryly.

"So why is mender mender? Over there, the robot's imp."

Jack let his breath out. mender gave a little beep, swiveling its lenses toward her.

"Perhaps we should have you list every power you know, once we're safe. There might be a pattern, and a clue in it."

Thunder rumbled. Over the mirrored HQ, a stygian cloud, lit with lightning flashes, loomed.

"So Captain Gale has come to rage." Jack frowned. "It seems natural for him. But I don't remember his ever having done it before—" He shook his head.

"Parallel histories," said Helen. "It had to make the worlds reflections of each other, which made things insane. You probably had more burglars than honest workers—but how could those few honest workers make enough to support themselves and all those burglars as well?"

mender meeped, thoughtfully.

Jack grimaced.

"You're different now," said Helen. "Phoebus would never dress like that."

He lifted an eyebrow. "Hiding?"

"Phoebus? Hide?"

After a moment, she glanced at the HQ. "That might not be Captain Gale."

Jack snorted. "Who else?"

The winds were reached out, whipping toward them, pulling on her hair and Jack's. "Sanddollar."

"She wouldn't—" said mender.

"Wouldn't she? Fomenting conflict?"

mender made little noises, and Helen wondered if it were pondering that.

"Then," said Jack, "we had best scout on the way by. So as to know." The wind whipped his hair back from his stern expression. "It is indeed just the sort of thing she would do."

***

The thunderhead loomed larger and larger. She felt it rising as well as saw it. The tiny figure in it came clear enough for her to be sure: Captain Gale.

"He's never done that before," said mender.

"Ours would never have tried," said Helen. "Even with his name."

Jack's breath hissed out. His hand stabbed through the air, picking out spots on the earth with the beams. Corpses lay about. Some wore costumes she could recognize, even blood-splattered. Some lay in such a way that the kill had to been mutual.

She shuddered. Sealing up the place and letting the slaughter proceed to the end might be their only choice. "I hope they took no prisoners."

"Prisoners?" A mad cackle greeted her—and a swirl of violet shadows. A pale avid face appeared in their dark heart. Mistress Twilight's lips pulled back from her teeth as if she would tear their throats out. Helen felt a little startled that she did not have fangs.

"As if prisoners mattered at all! When I have mastery of shadows and so of the scene!"

Jack and mender both watched her with a wary eye. Helen hardly dared to move. This Mistress Twilight was not so reserved as the original.

She could only hope that she would reveal her nefarious plans in what looked like vanity. . . .

She wished Shade were here, but she suspected she had only her companions. She hoped Jack knew that the brighter the light, the sharper the shadow.

"Prisoners," said Mistress Twilight scornfully. She jerked up shadows from the earth. They had enveloped six—seven—eight figures. Some were ordinary civilians in plain clothes—an elderly businessman, looking resigned; a young man in paint-splattered blue jeans; a terrified red-haired girl—but one wore the gaudy harlequinesque get-up of Puck.

Without the mischievous expression she was used to. Then, even the original Puck might look troubled with Mistress Twilight's feral gloating over them.

"Why have I kept my powers so secret before?" she mused.

Because, thought Helen, you would have changed history and acted nothing like the original, the solitary, the reserved Mistress Twilight. She started to summon the fog again. More diffuse this time.

"Never again, never ever shall anyone not know of my might!"

At least her musing kept her wrapped up in herself—instead of wondering why Sanddollar had turned quiet and retiring. The fog seemed to glow. She thickened it, and it clearly glowed. She glanced sideways. Jack's mouth moved in a tiny little curve of a smile—too little to be noticed by the woman gloating before them. She let out her breath slowly. Jack had realized. She looked back to the woman.

Mistress Twilight had always been careful, attentive, the first to notice any trick, and the only question was, as whiteness engulfed her, how quickly she would note that such flat light cast no shadows. All the more when it actually glowed from within and did not just seem to. . . .

"I shall call myself the Queen of the Night!"

The old man gave a choked cry. mender darted forward, metal limbs flaring outward, to catch all eight prisoners falling from broken shadow bonds. Helen sent the biggest gust of wind she could summon quickly into Mistress—the Queen's face. The Queen tumbled into the mists, only screaming in rage when the fog half-hid her—as if her failure did not dawn on her before then.

Jack set the fog ablaze with light about the Queen. Helen jerked her face away, blinking and tearing up from the radiance.

"This way!" she called, and flew.

***

The line appeared ahead—amazing how clear it was, with only the shift in lighting—and Helen felt the relief surge through her, all the more as she picked out figures flying patrol about her home.

She reminded herself that they were not safe yet. Had to reach them. Had to let them know that Jack and mender and the new Puck were all safe—

It did not calm her excitement. Neither did glancing sideways at the freed prisoners in mender's mechanical arms, still shocked and quiescent from their ordeal, too dazed even to ask questions about Sanddollar among their rescuers.

Past mender, Jack glanced back anxiously. She paused in her thoughts and started to turn, when a buffet of wind struck her like a mace, sending her tumbling through the air—and giving her a clear view of a towering thunderhead behind them. The charcoal gray clouds loomed against the sky, and rain fell in such torrents that she could see nothing under the clouds. Lightning laced through them, brilliant and ice-white. A bone-deep rumble followed so swiftly she could not mark a time.

She stilled the air as best she could, but this storm had been raised for a long time; inertia stood against her. Even the Weatherman could not put this one down quickly (and he would throw a fit on the effects it would have on weather patterns). Her mouth tightened, and she drew the stillness as close to the three of them as possible.

"mender, get the prisoners out. We'll follow as soon as we can."

She turned back without looking to see if she was obeyed. Soothing, her powers went out, instructing air and wind and water to calmness, but even the mistress of the seashore could only dispute such a storm and all its power; it would not dissolve into nothingness. She reached out trying to find the heart of the storm as it surged forward to loom over her.

The clouds started to glow. She blinked. Jack, next to her, shrugged and continued to illuminate. She stilled the air between them, so they could speak properly.

"If it's no help—" he said, raising an eyebrow.

"Some," she said, "but a little less would help more." He shrugged, the light slackened, and she tried to identify currents based on where the light shone through.

"What fool stunt—!" The sound, as much manipulated air as lungs, boomed out more loudly than the thunder. Helen forced her attention back to the storm. This time, her pushes moved it apart more readily—and a silhouetted figure flew from it toward them.

Jack held up his hand warily.

Captain Gale glared at him. "You fool! You think you have found yourself an *ally* in Sanddollar?"

Light lanced through the air, and Captain Gale staggered back, his clothes scorched.

Jack's voice came clearly. "I think she's found one in me."

"Sanddollar the queen of conflict? Who's always had it in for *you*? She'll turn on you for a joke and say it will just make you stronger—"

Helen drew a deep breath and tore. The storm shattered into a thousand pieces. Little clouds, no longer feeding on each other, either merely rained, or dissolved altogether.

Captain Gale, gaping, turned from Jack. The original would never have been so foolhardy. She gathered up the winds, whirling them about to mix up the air and even out the temperature. Even Captain Gale could not quickly gather a storm without shifting them apart again.

"Surrender and get it over with," said Jack.

Captain Gale's face contorted. "To you two? Neither of you can contain me, and if your *ally* is as weak as you are, Phoebus, she will not kill."

He flew for the line of the reflection. Not so fast as his reflection. For whatever reason.

Helen grabbed her phone and called for aid.

"A copy of Captain Gale—dangerous, maybe lethal—"

A swarm of heroes rose from beyond the reflection. At this distance, they could be nothing more than a cloud as ominous as locusts. Captain Gale veered off, inland, and flew lower. She opened her mouth to report it, but a sudden, sharp downdraft bore him downward. Unnatural, she felt in the air—and then it hurled him against a mine, and noise and flying blood burst outward.

She swallowed, hard. At least her stomach was already empty.

Part III

Mistress Twilight appeared, midair, before them almost before they crossed the line.

"Have you got somewhere I could hide?"

Helen opened her mouth, shut it again, and eyed the woman, whose grim face looked almost green.

"They need me here." She sounded forlorn. "They need access to my powers, and my knowledge of them, to help those poor souls. But they can't—they—"

Horror twisted her face. "One of them passed out at the sight of me. I—"

Not my bedroom, thought Helen, on a reflex. And told herself it was because if all the heroes tramped in and out of the room, it would be impossible to keep the rescued captives from seeing Mistress Twilight as long as they were here. That was the last finished room. Then—

"There's the basement," said Helen, neutrally. "Not much for rooms, but plenty of space. You could set up spellwork there." She thought of the stairways. And she guessed where they had put the captives of the Queen of the Night. "There's a small window into it. Can you look in and send yourself in?"

Mistress Twilight nodded. And seemed to notice Jack for the first time. He looked back. Helen wondered how he kept from tensing, when he would remember about the Queen of the Night under her old name,

46

but he remained serene. All three of them flew down, evading the line of sight of windows.

She hoped the debriefing was boring. Dull. Mind-numbing in its lack of incident.

Mistress Twilight glanced in the window, and moments later, appeared inside like a blossoming black flower. Helen circled around the house toward the door and saw Dr. Althea unloading her diagnostic machine.

Althea waved. "So this is the other Phoebus?"

Jack flushed a little. She looked him up and down, critically.

"He's last on the list. I have to see to the captives first. But I'll want to check him, too."

Jack did not move at all in mid-air. Helen scowled.

"The reflected doctors over there—the powers, and the mundane ones—they would have had to heal people to keep things parallel—" Her voice failed as she tried to imagine.

"They did not have patients," said Jack, quietly. "They had specimens."

Helen flinched.

"Ah—did I ever treat you over there?" said Dr. Althea.

Jack shook his head.

"There's that, at least."

***

After a clean bill of health, Puck sat quietly in the middle of the room, shaking a little, even with the blanket she had found about him, and the cup of bouillon. Having managed to ask them to call him Caleb.

Not having managed to devise a new code name on the fly, thought Helen. Then, the rest of Mistress Twilight's captives were, with the same blankets and hot drinks, were equally shaken, except for the little red-haired girl, who had somehow managed to fall asleep. Someone had carefully slipped her drink to the floor beneath her right hand. She was the only one among them to have used her right.

mender hovered over them like a mother hen not knowing how to aid her chicks, but they gave the robot wary glances now and again, to be reassured of its presence.

Jack sat off in a corner. Having found him relatively coherent, all the leaders wanted to question him for what he knew, though they seemed to be winding down.

She herself reached for another cup of bouillon, taking care not to glance at anything that would reflect her. She had enough horrified glances to say she was as pale as a ghost. Low-voiced discussion of the former captives and the villainous powers, and what to do, rumbled all around. She sipped at the cup. No one discussed how murderous the other Sanddollar had proven.

"How did you gain your powers?" asked Argent, gleaming even inside the house, his gaze intent on Jack.

Jack looked at his cup, in his left hand. "I was—a being hard to see, because too bright to look at, gave me a globe, and told me I would be interesting with it. It dissolved into my hands."

Helen remembered her own moment in that strange corner of shore, where a gleaming sphere of sea-green had appeared before her, and let her take it in hand. That had started her powers.

For some reason, the powers in the room seemed to have found that story more interesting than everything else he had said. They watched, openly or covertly.

"Is that supposed to be *opposite*?" said Mistral, her lip curling. "Just *interesting*?"

"We don't know what such a figure told Phoebus," said Captain Gale. "And finding a hero interesting is the opposite of finding a villain such."

"Wasn't much of a hero," said Jack. "Never could do much good." His mouth twisted. "Well, remembered good. Too weak to face them down."

Captain Gale went back to interrogating him about the details of the villains, in search of discrepancies, and Helen looked away.

Outside, the sky bore only wispy whiteness in cloud against the blue sky. No one had yet to mention how furious the Weatherman would be about the storm, either. Lucky Jake grumbled, with sidelong glances at the rescued, that they had never managed to make charges stick against the originals. Her mouth twisted. No judge would allow them to admit the virtue of the reflection as evidence in court. (And she still wondered who had dug up the reports that the unreflected girl was a heartless bully, and left-handed, and how.)

She drained her cup. The line of reflection had demarked where the powered guards and press began. Her house bustled with more people than it had ever seen before, over the years. Off in a corner, Jack disclaimed responsibility for the rescues until he blushed: mender and Sanddollar did the brunt of it, and could have managed without his help. From the intent expressions of the powers about him, any attempt to rescue him would be futile, winding down or not.

At least the press was not actually in the house. She went over to the TV, in the back room. A city scene showed two flares of pink: one Butterfly being dragged out on a stretcher, her glassy eyes staring at the ceiling, an IV dripping drugs into her arms, and another kneeling by a child, holding her hand and speaking in a low voice.

"Kid looks dazed," said Geometry.

"Oh yeah," said Wolfe, his eyes narrowed and his gaze fixed on her tiny televised mouth. "She's telling the kid that she's keeping him from getting upset until he's safe in the hospital, because it's dangerous."

The announcer said, "Rampant speculation connects this mysterious new Butterfly figure with the mysterious occurrences at the shoreline, but police have refused to make a statement about either issue, let alone any connection. This incident is the first time a victim of Butterfly's has been recovered without serious injuries, and among the few survivors."

"That shows the world the essence," said Jack, by her shoulder. She blinked. Must have been winding down more than she knew.

"There's little else to be learned about that." Jack jerked his thumb toward the reflection.

"Except who's been reflected. And the corpse count. And how it happened, and how it works, and whether it can happen again."

The last made Jack scowl fiercely.

"It's the chess masters," said Geometry dryly. He was, as always, focusing his eyes past the walls in consideration of the mathematics of the place, but he went on. "Anyone with any sense knows that, and that it can happen again but won't because they never repeated themselves."

The television blared on, oblivious. "—the only information from the shoreline is this shot, with Sanddollar in unaccustomed action. What is more, it shows her mysteriously accompanied by Phoebus and imp, in the process of evacuating people from an unknown location.

"Which raises many questions. Has Phoebus been recaptured? Has the notoriously vain, arrogant, and cruel supercriminal turned over a new leaf? Is there a reason why his notorious enmity to the reclusive Sanddollar has ceased?"

Jack grimaced and turned away, announcing that he was growing hoarse and needed to rest. Helen slipped over to suggest that he should have something to eat, and the kitchen was that way.

By that doorway, he stopped, glanced about, and said, very low, "Phoebus has it in for you."

Helen nodded, quickly, studying his face. The powers coming in glanced over, but without much interest.

He let his breath out. "*She* has it in for me. She's never told me why."

"Oh, it's the light powers," said Helen. "I have a vulnerability to them. . . ."

He stared at her.

"Look at the scene outside. I can control everything in it *except* the sunlight. Or any light that shines on it." Her hand swept the air. "Outside the seashore, apparently. But it influences the shore. A lot. And so it can harm me badly."

He snorted. "Wouldn't that make her *stronger*? To fight me more? Rather than to evade me?"

"I evade him," said Helen. "It had to mirror." She laid a hand on his arm, and plucked at her shirt with her free hand, the shirt that no longer looked like what the other woman wore. "Remember she doesn't have to reflect me anymore. You will be in danger if she decides to change that."

He scowled in thought.

"There's food if you're hungry."

She headed into the kitchen, where only half a dozen of the powers stood about, eating. At least they had brought supplies.

Northstar explained how, when Shade had reported that the shadowy mists had no magical shadows to them, he had gone into the mists at the edge of the reflection. As deeply as he could. He never lasted more than five minutes before finding himself turned around and coming back out.

"With absolute direction?" said Bluejay. "How does it *feel*?"

He spread his hands. "Only when I come out does it occur to me to wonder. It's as if it were numbed, and I was numbed from noticing."

Sounds like an excellent reason to avoid the mists, thought Helen, and headed for the supplies. The heroes' gazes went past her, to Jack. Who, after a moment, looked back, steadily. They muttered excuses and left the room.

"I hope they exhaust their fascination with a modest Phoebus soon." His gaze went to the window and the house's reflection, and he scowled. They had been questioning him during all the plotting, she remembered.

Quickly, Helen said, "We're blasting in as soon as the heavy-hitters arrive. Save any survivor who was prudent enough to hide well. Randomly risking ourselves would be folly."

Their supplies, she noted, included those liquid field rations meals. Better than anything she had—she doubted Jack would appreciate a cooked meal when fighting might erupt any time the reflected powers chose.

Jack snorted, but took the meal. "I wonder if we can search according to your side's knowledge of how imprudent they are. Since their history was so mirrored."

"I doubt it," said Helen, leaning on the counter. "Your Sanddollar was zealous about conflict, but she didn't turn into a socialite. She still is fond of her solitude." She colored a little. "Even over-fond."

"Not so much a virtue," said Jack. "If good is evil, and evil is good. . . ." He spread his hands.

Helen paused. "My opposite," she said slowly, "is not a drunkard or a glutton just because I am neither."

"Perhaps that would have changed history."

"So might imprudence." She sighed, and then her mouth twisted. "Now, of course, she can booze and gobble to her heart's delight, just as she is free to unleash chaos on the world, to foment conflict. She can do either, even if she did do only one."

Jack pondered a moment. "Is your Phoebus a drunkard?"

"Not at all. And Puck was a diligent burglar, and imp a diligent troublemaker." She waved a hand to where Cal, though still pale, had risen and spoke with Wolfe. "Despite his suffering, despite his obvious fear of a man he knows as violent and cruel—that man is hardly lazy. Or murderous, for that matter—Puck studiously avoids violence."

Jack studied the two men, talking. "What's the Golden Man like in your world?"

"Greedy," said Helen. "Greedy as all get out. And yours?"

"Steals from those with too much gold," said Jack. "To show them that life is more than money. He's perfectly sincere about it. Surrenders to do his time because it gives him a chance to speak. Though no one listens." He frowned.

"He's not in the reflection," said Helen. "Too far off in jail."

"Like a mirror," said Jack. "Right to left switch, not top to bottom. Or, actually, back to front." She glanced at him. "It's light, I studied it."

He took a swig from the package. "Though the reflections of the brave here never seem to be cowards there."

"Then, they do seem to be foolhardy," said Helen. Jack eyed her. "All virtue is the midpoint between two extremes and courage is between foolhardiness and cowardice."

"If that were so, the brave would stay brave, the cowards would be foolhardy, and the foolhardy cowards." Jack pondered a moment. "Insofar as it reflected as neatly as a mirror." He flattened the package, squeezing the last of it out the top.

The noises about the house seemed to subside. The television had someone talking about how powers could not be trusted, they were obviously a trick of those "philosophers" like all the others; they had been given the Ring of Gyges, and with that impunity, they could do all kinds of evil.

Even though they did not all become invisible, thought Helen, and dropped the package in the trash. He should try judging a tree by its fruit. But that thought did not erase the bitter note that reminded her that he was right; they could be very dangerous.

Shouts of greeting came from outside. Helen glanced through the window. Paladin swooped in from the mirrored side on his golden steed that galloped through the air without wings, and as Captain Gale went to meet him, dismounted. The horse dissolved into air. Helen put down her cup. Daystar or Arete might have been better for the fights that likely lay before them, but Paladin could help more with the survey, and was no slouch in a fight.

She did not feel surprised when Jack followed her out.

"Ah, Sanddollar," called Paladin. "You did nothing about that chapel?" He raised an eyebrow.

Everyone looked at her. Helen blushed.

"Nothing," she said firmly. "Not even look too closely."

For a moment, Paladin's face twisted. Then—"Prudent of you. I wished I hadn't." He turned to Captain Gale. "Mistress Twilight will be of little aid with it. You'll want to get Magister and Doctor Hermetic to check it. And someone from the church. And then Caryatid."

Captain Gale looked dubious.

"Once Caryatid has it down," said Helen firmly, "I can erode away the ruins." She would have to. With the interior hidden from the mirror, she did not want to think what sort of sorcery inspired Paladin to ask for those two powers.

Everyone looked at her again.

Jack shifted forward, to stand beside her. "On the bright side, Caryatid, Magister, and Doctor Hermetic were too far away to be reflected. You wouldn't want ours."

Paladin studied him.

"That's the place to start searching," said Captain Gale.

"Not for whatever the chess masters used?" said Jack.

She had not realized how many people had talked or done something that made sound. Even the air fell still. Then she realized that she had stilled it herself in her shock. She let out her breath with a gush and freed the air, telling herself not to be a fool. Jack knew more about the chess masters than they did.

The loosed air rustled grass, tugged at Jack's pale hair where he stood, and carried no sounds of voices.

Jack glanced about only long enough to see them all staring at him, studied the sand at his feet, and blushed.

And needed prompting. "Use?" said Helen. "They use things?"

"Always," said Jack. "They showed us when they did things—even when the time they had those hippopotamuses appearing in rooms—and explained why—" He glanced about. So many disbelieving stares came back that he fell silent.

"One of those reflected things," said Helen dryly. "They don't talk much here." The virtue of silence, she thought, and then—"Between their arrogance and their Olympian disdain, they would never explain a thing to us."

"*Ever*," said Wolfe with passion.

"So much for the theory," said someone, sotto voce, "that our chess masters really secretly mean us well."

Jack hesitated. "Mine do not really exist." His voice turned dry. "You would have noticed them. I did not really talk with them, or meet with them, or ever be in one of their philosophical worlds—I was created with my memories."

"Reflected memories," said Captain Gale. "You will tell everything you remember, even if it did not happen."

***

Helen hovered, by the window. Light drifted in about the table where Jack sat, and the powers gathered around him, recording.

He hardly need her help as he recounted how the world of paper had been a sheet of paper; the naked qualia, a prism; the naked extension, a filter; the hippopotamuses, toy ones. Within minutes, Captain Gale had sent every speedster he could find, and any other power who could search usefully, to look for a mirror out of place.

"The source of their powers is the gems on their wrists, the ones held on by those metal bands." Jack blinked. "And someone is meddling with light about here. The sort of thing I would do if I wanted to sneak about unseen."

Captain Gale sighed, pulled out his phone, and sent out an alert about Phoebus, probably invisible.

Jack slumped back in his chair. "That's everything the chess masters told me about what they did." His eyes unfocused. "Their explanations were less clear. I remember they were trying to enlighten us—but I think—" His tongue touched his lip. "I think that was one of the things where the reflection couldn't manage." He glanced about the milling powers. "Making things opposite there would have changed too much to be a reflection."

Captain Gale ran his hand through his hair. After a moment, he said, "I need to collate what the scouts are saying."

"You need to decide whether you're going to field this other Phoebus first," said Daedalus, his voice deep and sour. "Getting out of the reflection, he can plead necessity, but if you want him flying into the fray, he needs to register. He's not Phoebus, and Phoebus never registered, anyway."

Silence for a second.

"You'll need a new name," said Helen. "Jack is too encompassing."

"And they probably won't approve something so simple as Bright," grumbled Jack.

That must have mirrored the same. "You just have to phrase it right," she said. "Radiance. Resplendence. Refulgence—"

"Jack Bright," said Jack, firmly. "A compound will pass."

Daedalus mentioned paperwork, and Captain Gale's phone rang. After a moment, he turned on the news. Helen blinked. If it were in the news already, it would have to be major.

An excited young woman and man babbled at a TV camera, telling how Phoebus had raged at a public TV and said that if Sanddollar thought she could get allies from this magic mirror, she'd find that he had tricks, too. More witnesses followed, until it dawned on her—

"He—" said Helen. "He thinks that if I hate him, the mirror must mean that my reflection adores him." And her gaze went to the house that reflected hers.

"I felt him," said Jack. "He must have slipped by."

"Slip?" jeered Wolfe. "Phoebus?"

"He wants his adoring Sanddollar," said Jack.

***

In the gap as the strike team assembled, Caryatid and Daystar came soaring over the dunes to land before the porch, to Helen's relief. Even if

Caryatid's first question was whether the interiors matched, and she had to admit that she did not know.

"Like Alice. Or, rather, Through the Looking Glass—everything that's visible in the mirror is reflected the same. Past it—" She spread her hands. "The house looks the same, but so does the land about, and the mines were a bit hard to miss once Lucky Jake walked out there."

Daystar's gaze shifted to Jack. Who shook his head.

"I was her nemesis there, as he was hers over here, but I was never inside." His mouth twisted. "Thus far, I've never been inside a place both there and here—even in false memory."

"Time's a-wasting," said Captain Gale. "We need to move. Jack, can you hide us all? Or redirect any lasers?"

"Both," said Jack, cheerfully, walking down the porch stairs and glancing about the team. "Give me a sec."

At least, thought Helen, the reflection had not turned Phoebus's arrogance into mock modesty. The air about them seemed to shimmer, and settle down.

"The trick," said Jack, "is letting us see, and see each other, and transmit light to hide us. *He*'ll be able to sense us, but not just where we are."

Captain Gale nodded. "Warn us if you feel him hiding. Sanddollar, check the environs—let us know what you sense, and where we can land."

Helen nodded.

"Can you get rid the landmines?" said Daystar.

"Yes," said Helen. Daystar had the least to fear, being invulnerable, as well as strong, which was just as well. "But I couldn't do it so she wouldn't notice. I would have to trigger them, not disable them. She'd notice. So would he. I can pick out a safe route, though."

Her thoughts roved ahead, picking through the granules, and she managed to keep from wincing. Yes, she could. It would not be easy. "All the other doors are traps," she said. "The front door you can still go in and out of—assuming she doesn't put the traps inside."

"To the front door, then," said Captain Gale. "Jack keeps us invisible, Caryatid checks and takes the door down, or the wall if necessary—as little as possible—we search the place, and both Phoebus and that Sanddollar get taken down on sight." He glanced sideways. "Jack Bright and our Sanddollar stick with me."

Helen nodded, sharply, and drew a deep breath. She felt the plants, the sand, the breezes, and could make out her companions even without Jack's work, by the gap they left as they flew over the dunes. None of the lasers fired, but as they approached, some began to smoke. She stirred the sand, a little, about them, to stifle the fire. They settled on the porch, soft footfalls sounding. Caryatid strode up to put her hands to the lintel, and Daystar hovered beside her, anxious because her skills were little use in battle—

Helen glanced at Jack. She would have to ask him how Caryatid and Daystar had met and married in the reflection. When a villain had knocked out structural support for a building, to leave Daystar the futile task of saving as many as he could while the villain escaped—and a woman, Mette, had stepped out of the crowd to save the building and all within, letting Daystar snag the villain. She had said afterward that she had been given a strange globe like marble and told she would know when to use it, and had become Caryatid on the spot. Helen let her breath out. She could not even imagine a villainous version—

"In," said Caryatid, breaking into her thoughts. The air cracked as the door crumbled. Lasers whirred as they turned, and did not fire. Smoke rose, and she stifled more of it. The other powers piled inside, and she scrambled after, into a room quite as large as her own main room.

"No sign of life," said Daystar.

"We saw her go in," said Captain Spark. "And not out. And we've had it under surveillance every millisecond."

Helen shrugged. "Sand's not disturbed—she didn't tunnel out."

"And I'm not finding anything, either," said Caryatid. Lucky Jake called Wolfe over to her bedroom, to smell out any trace. Helen looked away. The decor had been exactly like hers, but the other Sanddollar had started to tear it down. As ill-suited, no doubt.

"I can't feel anyone shifting light, either," said Jack.

"Basement, then," said Helen. "Geometry would have picked up if she had any dimensional tricks, and without that, I'd hide there."

Jack grinned. "Let's hope she'll do the same—that that's not reflected."

Captain Gale gave him a baneful glance and assigned Cherubim and Wolfe to guard the way up, Daystar to take one group down the back stair, and he himself to take the front stair.

When she reached the bottom, she glanced about the narrow corridor. "It looks like the same positions of doors and walls, but it's made of sterner stuff. Don't try to blast through unless you have to."

Wolfe sniffed, audibly. "Can't smell through 'em."

"May be nothing to smell," said Captain Gale. "Move out."

Helen lingered at the tail end, feeling the sands about the basement, and vaguely, the walls and doors. Guards on the stairs were all very well, but she could burrow out at any time. So could her reflection.

Door after door was slid open, and the rooms behind pronounced clear. There was not, after all, that much to search, even when they checked with powers.

Then Jack pulled open a door to reveal scarlet. Even she could smell inside, and everyone turned toward it. In spite of herself, she took a step toward it and got a clear view.

Jack yanked her away, glanced about, and dragged her into the lower bathroom.

Miserable minutes later, Jack handed her a glass of water to wash out her mouth. Outside, the talk revolved about whether, between the burning with light beams and the sand-blasting to pieces, whether they could really be certain these were Phoebus and the other Sanddollar, and if it were possible to test the DNA of their reflections to be sure.

"First of all remove the bodies," said Captain Spark. "Send for some coffins."

Helen headed for the stairs by the route that did not take her past the door. She hoped one of the powers had the power to scrape those ruins into a coffin.

Part IV

Pastel sunset colored the sky and sea, and returning powers were silhouetted against it, carrying this passenger, and that prisoner. Fewer as the sky darkened from peach and rose to flame and scarlet shades.

At the table inside, Caryatid played solitaire, only now and again looking up and out the window. Helen could not have managed it. Certainly she could not have slept, like Jack sprawled on the couch. Even the thought of sleeping brought back the nightmarish memories of that room—

She shivered and turned back to monitoring sand and wind and wave, seeing that no one slipped by. With the other Sanddollar gone, and so many other powers dead, escape had grown more difficult for anyone plausible, but it was still worth watching for them.

Time inched by.

Every now and again, she caused fountains of sand to spurt, testing her abilities. She could not sandblast the way the other Sanddollar had, though even this little practice improved it.

Caryatid stood up and stretched, walked about the room a bit, and finally came out on the porch.

"I hope you don't find it too wearisome," said Helen.

Caryatid shook her head. "Makes me understand why you live out here. Why some powers want to build enclaves of safety and only commute to cities."

A minute later, she went back to the game, and Helen went on with her practice.

Jack roused at some point, moved about the room, settled down in a corner. When she finally stirred and went in, he bent over an old book of hers, one an aunt had bought to teach her how to draw. He certainly got more use out of it than she ever had, by the pencil marks on the papers beside him. The landscapes even looked recognizable to her.

Then he threw down his pencil and scowled before stretching and muttering that it could not show the light.

"It could be a long time before they find the mirror," he said.

Helen nodded.

"I should have sketched outside, by the sunlight." His gaze went to the windows, where sunset was still visible. "I knew it might take a long time to find that mirror."

A squad of powers flew by. From the flare of shadows, they had just captured the Queen of the Night. Then, both Shade and Mistress Twilight had been on that assignment.

"*She's* going to be hard to keep captive," said Jack, sourly.

"I wonder if the chess masters timed it, to select the powers to appear. To make the reflection work better." She glanced back at Caryatid and scowled. "There's no Daystar, or Caryatid, over there, but—you remember them, don't you?"

"Daystar was a violent, selfish, greedy monster, and Prankster once had to upend a building on him to escape, but a woman, Mette, came out of the crowd, out of nowhere, to become Caryatid on the spot and hold it up for him, so that he could catch—" Jack shook his head.

"Prankster was a problem. Seven powers, no less, emerged at times and places where it seemed clear they were aimed at containing him. Mette became Caryatid as the last of them, to hold up that building—but since Daystar would sacrifice his chance to catch Prankster to save people, why didn't yours just drop it and let the people die?"

Jack spread his hands.

"Then Daystar and Caryatid married within a year. They have five children, and are very happy. How could yours get along any more than—" She felt her face starting to heat, but she would look even sillier to not say it. "—our Phoebus and your Sanddollar?"

"A chance to exploit each other, maybe." Jack sighed. The sky was turning violet and deepest crimson. His voice grew softer. "Why violence? There are other evils. Why that one?"

"Perhaps they were most interested in powers," said Helen. "If the heroes become villains, and the villains become heroes, the most signal differences between the powers is willingness to use violence."

Jack ran a hand through his hair. "That—would explain it."

Then, in the twilight, Mistress Twilight appeared. "Where is Captain Gale? We have the mirror."

Part V

Captain Gale double-checked the evacuation of the reflection, and set the guards to ensure that no one could drift in while the powers acted. Stars appeared in the sky by the time he was done, but then, he had no choice. Who could tell what the reflection would do when the mirror was interfered with?

Especially now, with the sands outside lit up by lights from her home, shining on Mistress Twilight conferring in a low voice with Magister and Dr. Hermetic, and another power whom Helen thought was named Sorcienne. All the other powers, like her, hovered around uselessly, waiting for the moment when those four would speak and give them tasks, for now able to do nothing but stay out of the way.

"Jack Bright," said Sorcienne, looking up. The light cast sharp, distorting shadows on her face. "Do they have ways to see through any screen we put up? Analysis may take some time, and if they realize what we are doing—"

Jack closed his eyes, and his hand ran through his hair. The night wind blew by.

"They never said." He opened his eyes. "They tried to help us, reflected. They would not have been such fools as to confide anything that would help the brutes and monsters in anything but reform."

"You and Sanddollar—her for mist, you for light, to direct it away—that would make the most natural looking shield."

Helen grimaced. The Weatherman would not like it, but he probably already detested the storm, and the chess masters' works had angered him before. She nodded.

"Lead on, Mistress Twilight," said Jack. "We should probably have the shield up before the force arrives."

Helen's thoughts went out, searching the scene. At least at night, raising mist came more easily, if not wholly naturally.

"I can direct the light to let us see to walk," said Jack.

***

Walk and not much more, thought Helen. Not even see things in color.

Trees grew on the hillocks below—pines, all of them, but growing straight and not twisted and bent by the sea winds. Light glowed, down the shore, but not so near as she would expect—on a normal day, with no reason to evacuate.

The pine-scented breeze, almost chilly, blew by her.

"Here," said Mistress Twilight, softly. They settled to the ground in a meadow hollow. A mirror stood there, barely visible in the light Jack gave. Taller than a human and just as wide. She could not see herself in the reflection from where she stood. Or, in this gloom, the grass or wildflowers, or the trees that edged this hollow. She drew a deep breath. With no water about, either standing or running, to make her task easier. She closed her eyes.

"The mists?" said Mistress Twilight.

"It's coming, it's coming," said Helen. "It has to look natural if you want it to fool them. It will still come—and more quickly if I am not disturbed in the process."

A low laugh came out of the gloom—Jack, she thought. Helen screwed her eyes shut and tugged. Mist rose. From the ocean, from the streams, from the ponds, it thickened in the air and seeped over the land. She let her breath out and opened her eyes.

"How far will it reach?" said Mistress Twilight.

"Seems a natural distance now. Easier to maintain if I don't spread it farther.

"Then we're ready." Jack shone a little more brightly. The flowers in the scrap of meadow took on colors; the trees were green needles above and amber ones on the forest floor. The mirror itself was straightforwardly square, held in a metal frame that had three layers, like steps, going down to the surface, which showed the grasses and flowers, the pines with curls of mist about them, Jack, Mistress Twilight, and her, looking very pale. Mists covered all else.

With vague thoughts of keeping out of the way, Helen edged to one side, where the mirror would no longer reflect her. Sorcienne, Dr. Hermetic, and the Magister appeared from the mists, and Jack joined her. Sorcienne started to lay mirrors about the meadow.

Helen started to turn her thoughts back to the mists, to feeling out any oddity in the land. Jack came out beside her.

"We can't be seen in the mirror here," he murmured.

"How sagacious of us," she whispered. "It can only help avoid another Phoebus, and another reflected Sanddollar—"

A flare of light before them silenced her. She flinched back, toward the pines.

"They seemed interested in work," said the red chess master, the voice deep, melodious. Inhuman faces turned toward them. Their gigantic bodies, floating in midair before the mirror, were thick, blockish, angular as if carved, uniform in color whether black or red. They could have either worn armor based on chess pieces, or been themselves chess pieces grown to enormous size and brought to life; as always, there was not the slightest clue which was the truth.

The black chess master swept the air with his hand. The three wizards froze in place.

"So unproductive an experiment," mused the red chess master. "So difficult to correlate the results."

Helen touched Jack's arm. It would be easier if they had Geometry with them—or had planned—but she tapped her wrist. Jack's eyebrows went up; the jewels could not be seen from they stood.

She pointed to the Sorcienne's mirrors.

For a moment, he looked blank. Then a smile crept onto his face, his hands went out and pointed, and two beams of light shot out, glanced from mirrors, and struck the chess masters' wrists full bore.

Her heart hammered out the moments. . . one. . . two. . . three. . . .

"So!" The chess masters spoke with one voice and wheeled on the two of them, so intent that the wizards gasped and moved behind them.

"Our little pair of oddities!" said the red one.

"You could not even manage to fight a team-up of your doubles," said the black one, severely. "That would have shown far more than your sulking off to evade them."

The air was very still about them. Helen realized she was hushing it and let her breath out. Then she left it hushed.

The red chess master snatched at the air, and Jack rose up as if pulled by a puppetmaster's string. "Jack Bright, who wants to be an artist. What sort of reflection is that?"

The ambient light glowed from the jewels. Helen drew a deep breath and let it out again. Keeping the air still, she reached out and felt sand. It drew nearer and gathered.

Jack bounced in the air as if tossed and caught. Helen bit her lip. A little more sand. . . .

"Whatever shall we do with you?" murmured the black chess master.

Sand surged from the surface, in two narrow beams. Helen put all her strength into their speed. Blasting, the sand struck the bracelets and tore at them, and Helen felt how it pried between the gems and the jewelry. Harder, she thought, forcing it onward.

"You fool!" Both spoke as one, and turned toward her, and Jack hovered in the air. Light blasted from his hands, hitting the jewels, and they shattered.

The chess masters plummeted to the ground. Still big and blockish, they stared at her.

Light cascaded about them as Jack illuminated the entire scene. The chess masters did not seem to care; they did not shift.

"What have you done, you fool?" said the red chess master.

"Do you not know they can not undo *our* handiwork?" said the black chess master. His hand swept toward the wizards.

"Only we can," said the red one.

"You mean," said Helen, coldly, "you will not make Jack wink out of existence, as well as in?"

"Of course," said the red chess master. "Obviously."

"Always before," said the black chess master, full of intensity, "we have cleaned up after our experiments. You have never had to suffer something lingering and causing problems."

Jack settled on the ground beside her. A burning desire to kick both chess masters boiled up, and she clenched her fists. As if that would penetrate their thick heads and hard hearts. She turned to Jack, caught his hand, and kissed him on the cheek.

"Such enthusiasm," said Mistress Twilight.

"And here," said Helen, "I thought you, of all women, could be counted on to have regard for privacy."

Dr. Hermetic cleared his throat. "Whatever shall we do with them?"

"Arrest them," said Helen.

"For what?" said the red chess master, sullenly.

"Conspiracy to murder Jack Bright will do to start with," said Helen, surprising herself with how sugary sweet she could make her voice. "We can follow that up with more charges."

"Does the grass arrest the elephant?" said the black chess master. "The elephant tramples it at will."

"Until we shoot it as a brute beast, incapable of reason." Helen turned to the others. "We have enough dead bodies from this alone that we could come up with a long list."

"When you did not even know where your powers came from," said the black one, his voice a deep rumble, full of fury. "Do you expect more powers to come forth to your aid?"

"We'll manage," said Captain Gale, dryly.

***

"Excellent job," murmured the Weathermaster, eyeing the shoreline. "Truly, I could not have done it better myself."

Helen reminded herself that they knew the Weathermaster had been too far away to have changed for a reflected version of himself.

"Won't do for the future, of course. I will need monitors all over this to scope out the effects on the weather patterns, and all over the world to detect whether something like this whenever it happens. Was a stopgap for desperation—"

Now, that sounded more like him. Helen pulled back and let an aide step forward to take notes. It was a lot easier to contain the Weathermaster now that he had people scurrying to tend to his rather eccentric needs.

She took off into the brilliant day. And it did help control the weather.

Soaring over the reflected town showed the pattern, how Caryatid had been uneven in pulling down the buildings. Some had been swallowed up by sand, and grass was already overgrowing those sites. Then, she had carefully avoided reading the reports on why Caryatid had torn down those sites specifically, though she had helped erode those that had been destroyed.

Past it stood the cemetery. The gravestones were flat to the ground, and marked with numbers, not names, but even so basic a burial ground had cost a pretty penny. Helen soared over it, circling about, trying to bring some order to her thought.

"Hullo!" Jack waved, and moments later, he had flown over to join her. His backpack was slung over one shoulder, but he did not look ready to sketch this scene.

"They never had a chance," said Helen.

Jack raised an eyebrow.

"The chess masters created them full of malice, rancor, and bitterness, and set them down where that would rebound as badly as possible, as quickly as possible. Many lived for only minutes. Some for only seconds. They never had a chance."

A breeze sprung up, and she shivered. The prosecutor was going for felony murder. She had already talked with the office several times about her own testimony. It did not console her.

"Now we see as through a mirror, darkly," said Jack. "Then we shall see face to face. . . ."

"Like their cave," said Helen, dourly.

"They thought they could fake Plato's cave, but they didn't really have anything transcendental to offer, outside it. That reflects on them, not on transcendence."

She nodded, slowly, and they flew on in companionable silence, until her phone rang its alarm.

Her mouth twisted. "I've got to get back. Caryatid is going to do the chapel this afternoon."

"Like the town?"

"Oh, we're doing it a bit more. You can come and watch, if you like."

"Why so much later?"

"Dr. Hermetic and Paladin insisted on being scrupulously and vigorously thorough with it before she did."

Jack opened his mouth and shut it again. He still flew alongside her.

***

Even at a distance, the changes were obvious. Parts of it were bleached to a snowy whiteness from whatever Dr. Hermetic and Paladin had done to purify it. The garden had been torn up, and every plant desiccated and burned. Some things had just been blasted away. It certainly seemed less creepily off than when she had first seen it.

She still settled on the sand dunes a fair distance from it.

Jack settled beside her. Caryatid was deep in discussion with Paladin, and her part would not come until she was done. She turned to Jack.

"So, how is art school coming?"

"I see what they mean by attractive nuisance," said Jack, ruefully, but then smiled. "But the classes are going well. Gawkers can't stop me from learning."

Caryatid nodded, decisively, and Helen could not look away. Caryatid walked over, put her hands to the main door, and closed her eyes in concentration. Over the next minute, creaks, groans, and cracks sounded over the sands. Then, abruptly, as supports gave way, wood and metal imploded inward, into a shattered heap. Which collapsed further, and shattered more. Minutes later, little of its original shape could be guessed.

Helen reached outward, into the sands and sea.

Caryatid stepped away and waved to Helen. Her voice carried as the little company walked toward her. "They said you would do more?"

"Already started." She pointed to the shore. Waves pounded on the sands, eating them away in a span about twice as large as the chapel, and eating inward.

"We'll have a bay here by the time you're done," said Jack.

"For a time," said Helen. "I don't think it will be stable. But at least the chapel will be scattered to the seven seas."

"Good thing, too," said Paladin. "Dr. Hermetic thought it might have evil potential in the hands of the misguided."

The waves pounded on.

"Did you hear about the new power? Up north?" said Paladin, casually. "A speedster."

Helen shook her head.

Dr. Hermetic chuckled. "The chess masters in their cells stopped trying to claim they were responsible for us, and would regret taking their powers, after that."

"And better news," said Caryatid, brightly. "About the pocket? Some people are thinking of building a town there."

"It would be inconvenient," said Helen, slowly. She herself had arranged only to acquire title to the reflection of her own property; they were outside it now.

"For some reasons," said Caryatid. "For powers, however—well, you don't live out here for nothing."

It would be close enough for her to train more. Mistral had been right in that, at least.

"Send roads down from the hills," said Paladin cheerily, "build docks, and, of course, many will fly in and out. And they can build schools and things with powers in mind."

"Sanddollar City," said Caryatid.

Helen blinked. "Oh no you don't, I didn't do anything that dozens of other powers didn't do."

Caryatid laughed. "You were the first."

"And Super City just sounds stupid," said Jack. "Or Bright City."

She rolled her eyes. "Hermit City, perhaps, because it's hidden away. You're not going to name it Chess Master City, at any rate."

Also by Mary Catelli

Curses And Wonders
Dragon Slayer
Eyes of the Sorceress
Fever and Snow
Mermaids' Song
Sword and Shadow
The Book of Bone
Witch-Prince Ways
Dragonfire and Time
Enchantments And Dragons
Jewel of the Tiger
Over the Sea, To Me
The Dragon's Cottage
The Maze, the Manor, and the Unicorn
The White Menagerie
A Diabolical Bargain
Madeleine and the Mists
Magic And Secrets
The Lion and the Library
The Princess Goes Into The Forest
The Wolf and the Ward
The Witch-Child and the Scarlet Fleet
Treachery And Spells
Winter's Curse
Crow Curse

Free Passage
Isabelle and the Siren
Journeys And Wizardry
Lifestone
Magic of the Lost God
Never Comment On A Likeness
One Name
The Drunken Mermaids
The Turtle in the Sea of Sand
Were I You
Where There Is Smoke
Through A Mirror, Darkly

www.ingramcontent.com/pod-product-compliance
Lightning Source LLC
Chambersburg PA
CBHW020641130626
46552CB00003B/1349